Young Cyrano

Paul Cicchini

One Knight Publishing LLC
ERUDITIONIS HONOREM
P.O. BOX 2072
VINELAND, NJ 08362

Young Cyrano

ISBN: 978-1-63795-354-9

Library of Congress Control Number 2018933237

Introduction

The first thing the reader needs to know is that Cyrano is not a fictional character. Savinien Cyrano de Bergerac actually lived in France in the 17th century (the early 1600s) and he did have a large nose that he was proud of, but it was never as huge and as grotesque as exaggerated in literature.

He is one of my heroes because he was a true Renaissance man. That is to say that he did not actually *live* during the Renaissance but that he was a well-rounded individual who was accomplished in many areas: arts, sciences, and warfare. He wrote books, plays, and poetry and conjectured about science. He had a wicked sense of humor and he was a renowned swordsman that reliable sources say took on one-hundred foes in a single night. It is not often that you find an individual who served gallantly in battle (the Siege of Arras) and also wrote romantic poetry.

Being a writer, behavioral scientist, fencer, martial artist, and character educator myself, you might say that I tried to emulate his example, and you would be right.

I have read several biographies on Cyrano as well as the famous account of Cyrano in Rostand's play of the same name (which also inspired several movies). I often wondered what happened in Cyrano's earlier life that inspired him to be such a rebellious, heroic, free-thinker who stuck to his principles and personal integrity even if it got him in trouble. I decided to craft a story based on my theories. *Young Cyra-*

no is loosely based on a collection of chronicles of Savinien Cyrano's life and my own imaginings. I rejected some unsubstantiated scandals, rumors, and innuendoes surrounding his legend, as I felt they didn't fit with the role model I had come to admire. I took many liberties in telling this tale, but still tried to be as historically faithful as I could.

I would also like for you to keep in mind that back in the Paris of 1633, "college" was actually what we would today call "high school" so that is why our Young Cyrano is enrolled there at the tender age of fourteen.

My sincerest hope is that this story will inspire you in four ways:

↘ To watch the original Rostand play *Cyrano de Bergerac* (particularly the version starring Peter Donat) so that you might know what a true classic is.

↘ To run to the closest history book to find out more about our past.

↘ To become a well-rounded person yourself.

↘ To be a person of good character.

Chapter 1

"Savinien...Savinien!"

Hercule-Savinien Cyrano clicked his tongue and ignored the silly girl calling him. His father was a rising star in France's royal court, and he had decided to show off his newfound favor in the Paulette government by acquiring househelp for their estate. Yvette, a girl only two years Cyrano's senior, was the first to be hired by Papa, and from day one, she made it her personal mission to boss him around like an old hen. Worse yet, she insisted on calling him by his 'baptized' name, Savinien (the same name as his grandfather), instead of his preferred name, Cyrano, thus annoying him to no end.

For this reason, and because he wished to return to his musings on the properties of the sky, he had no time for the vapid maiden. The county cloister where he studied dismissed in the summer when the heat became too oppressive. On the first day of a long solstice holiday from school, he would tolerate nothing spoiling his relaxation or rumination.

Cyrano always relished the summer break, not only because he could lounge barefoot under the cooling trees of *Domaine Bergerac* - his family's estate - but also because it freed his mind to ponder wildly fantastic ideas not entertained by Curate Berthault, the teacher in his church-run school.

Yvette continued to call for him with a pronounced note

of impatience in her strident voice. Cyrano blinked with languid ease as he considered the characteristics of the clouds that tooled by high above his favorite tree at the frontage of the estate. *What are they really made of?* One day, he would build something… a ship for the skies… or some other way to escape the ground and touch them to determine their true nature. Yes, an *airship.* If one could sail the seas on a vessel, there had to be a way to capture the power of the wind, escape the earth and ascend heavenward. *That's a good one. When I return to the house, I must find a quill and notebook and write that idea down.*

Just then, a fate far worse than Yvette disturbed his dream-voyage.

"Oy! You!"

Oh, what now? He pulled his eyes away from the clouds and trailed them earthward to discern the origin of this next interruption. Two older, rather large, dirty, slack-jawed, and shabbily dressed boys loomed ominously over him.

"Give us a *pistole* or some food, or we'll break your arm!"

This unfortunate turn of events made Cyrano jump involuntarily and launched a pool of fire in his stomach. It wasn't every day that sinister-looking boys came to the edge of his home to extort money.

Don't show fear, he coached himself. He knew he needed to control his emotions in order to emerge from this dangerous situation unscathed. He would have to employ his very agile brain and his even quicker mouth to talk his way out of this predicament. *I hope they're as dull-witted as they look.*

He found himself at a strategic disadvantage lying on the ground. That would have to be rectified. He breathed in deep and forced a friendly smile.

Make them believe you are harmless. Get their guard down.

"A *pistole* is a lot of money. What makes you think that I possess even a single white *franc,* let alone a *pistole,* my friend?" he said, feigning innocence.

"Because, *mon ami,* you are a rich boy from Gascony, and all rich boys have Spanish gold *pistoles,*" reasoned the remarkably ugly boy with a bowl haircut. His teeth jutted from various obtuse angles and the breath that wafted down from him was a mixture of metal and stale onions.

From Cyrano's lamentable and poor vantage point, he guessed this boy to be a full two inches taller than his criminal cohort, and obviously the leader of the two. *Time for a heavy dose of charm; and misdirection.*

"Well, I applaud your sharp eye for breeding, kind sir. I am indeed of noble birth…and delicate of constitution. I rest under this tree every day… to convalesce…from last winter's plague, which I barely survived!"

The two goons recoiled at the mere mention of the word "plague."

Good. There's my opportunity. He got up on one knee, but they closed in on him again before he could stand. Cyrano hid his quiet curse with a cagey smile and formulated another move. He pretended to search his body for something. "Now, if you would be so kind as to help me up, I will search for my purse. Perhaps you *should* be rewarded for your keen recognition of nobility. Oh, don't be afraid. That doctor with the funny beaked mask told my parents I was *barely* contagious…any more…"

He scrambled to his feet when the youthful hoodlums took two steps back at the word "contagious." Knowing his muggers would recover their ground in a blink, he made a rather ostentatious show of checking his person again.

"Oh, dear, it seems I have left my rather fat purse back at the *château*. Silly me!!" He threw up his hands in mock peevishness.

The lead bully wrinkled his freckled brow. Cyrano reckoned that the boy finally realized he was being mocked. "Odo, get him!"

The two young gangsters descended upon their prey, but Cyrano had home-field advantage. From years of summers clambering on the estate's trees, he'd developed skills of equal parts gymnast and chimpanzee. Arms still up, he jumped and reached for a familiar, low-hanging branch from his favorite tree and hoisted himself up. He was now high enough to swing and kick the fattest of the boys, Odo, in the stomach with both feet. When the thug doubled over in pain, Cyrano used his assailant's back to boost himself higher up the tree and out of harm's way-for now.

He could not resist the temptation to heckle his foes. He grinned and taunted them. "Foolish brigands! Oafish pirates! Well, I have neither gold, silver, nor even bread to give you…but how about some fruit?" He reached up and plucked a round, plump apple from a branch and threw it at the head of one of his jumping adversaries. Cyrano crowed in triumph. With air-superiority and plenty of edible ammunition, he could keep his would-be marauders at bay until reinforcements arrived- perhaps his father, or even that caterwauling Yvette. Finally, she would be of some use!

"Savinien!" Yvette's calls sounded very close now.

Ah, my shrill savior is at hand.

The boys froze for a brief moment at the cry. "Ruffe, what do we do?" Odo asked his leader.

"Let's get out of here!" Ruffe turned and bounded from the tree at full speed and down the dusty dirt road, away from the borders of the estate.

Sensing a complete victory, Cyrano hurled one final *fruit-grenade* and boinked the noggin of Ruffe as he ran away.

This last act of cockiness cost him dearly, though, because he lost his footing on the branch. He tumbled out of the tree, frontwards, smashing his face on a stump as he landed on the otherwise soft ground.

"Savinien!" Yvette gasped as she came upon the moaning boy and turned him over on his back. Cyrano felt blood matting his shirt to his skin, and his nose throbbed as it felt to him to treble in size through the pain.

"Oh, Savinien! Did those villains beat you?"

"No, you idiot! I beat *them*! A crushing victory mind you-- until you distracted me! And stop calling me Savinien, my name is *Cyrano*!"

At this, his eyes rolled back and his body went limp.

* * * *

"*Mon Dieu*! The master will beat *me* for letting you come to such harm. Ugh! You are too heavy for me to carry you home," Yvette bawled at the unconscious boy.

"Fear not, *Mademoiselle*. I shall help you get the boy home."

Yvette looked up from her weeping to find a gangly man in a tailored suit walking down the dirt lane towards her.

"Oh, *Monsieur*, it is all right. I will manage…" Yvette lowered her eyes and wrapped her arms around herself. She hoped she could dissuade him from coming any closer.

"*Mademoiselle*, I insist, or I shall have to relinquish any claim of being a gentleman," the man replied with a noble tone.

She studied him further. He appeared to be just a few years older than her, with a kind face. His attire and outward appearance portrayed that of a scholar, if only a humble one.

She finally nodded, and gave him a coy smile.

"Thank you. I could indeed use some assistance. Our *château* is nearly a tenth of a league away from this fence… *Monsieur*…?"

"Gassendi, *Mademoiselle*. *Professor* Pierre Gassendi," he said and bestowed her with a gallant bow.

Chapter 2

Cyrano awoke in the darkness of his own room. With the door slightly ajar even from his bed, he was aware of several voices emanating from downstairs. One he recognized as that of his father, Abel, but he could not place the voice of the other man.

Was he in trouble? He slid out of bed to hear better. *Ouch!* His head throbbed as if stuck inside the very bells of *Notre Dame de Paris* at vesper's call. And his nose - oh, his nose ached as if a Grand Inquisitor had laid a blazing iron upon it. He muffled a yelp of pain and crept towards the hallway to see.

"Again, Professor Gassendi, I cannot thank you enough for your kindness towards my maid and my son." Abel Cyrano, Lord de Bergerac, was a roundish man with a prosperous paunch. His center-parted hair and bristly moustache reminded people of an ornately-scrolled anniversary clock.

"Lord Bergerac, it was nothing, but as I have told you, my payment is that you allow me the honor of serving you and your family further- in return for a small patronage. Your boy is nearly eighteen and will be going to a college soon, no? He needs advanced instructions to be prepared for the demands of higher education. The kind that the county cloister cannot possibly offer him."

"Mmmph, you have a point there, Gassendi. He needs something more." Abel rubbed his chin and then brightened,

"Well, then it is settled, dear *Professor*. Starting tomorrow, Hercule will be your philosophic protégé and you will school him in the prosperous way of mathematics—"

"And science, Lord Bergerac. Let us not forget the value of the sciences!"

"Indeed, Gassendi, indeed," Abel stuck a thumb in his vest as he paced, "But if my son is to follow in my footsteps and continue the family service in the King's Ministry of Finance, he must know his numbers, too. Heheh."

Cyrano had reached the landing of the second floor and heard the end of the conversation. He could hold his tongue no longer. "Father! Not *another* school!"

"Hercule! I am relieved you are awake. Now, my son, you've been boasting to me for years that you are smarter than the priests at the *curé* and they can't teach you anything else. Well, now's your chance to prove it. Professor Gassendi here will prepare you for university. You need to learn how to be a nobleman. Someday, you can be a tax collector like me or Grandfather. Perhaps even continue my legal practice."

"Or perhaps a scientist," Gassendi interjected. "Oh dear," he gasped. "Your face looks no better than the last time I saw it."

"What? Oh, are you talking about the two shiners under my eyes, or my bloated nose?" Cyrano plopped down on the middle of the steps. "Father, I don't want to be a despised publican. I want to be a Musketeer."

"Nonsense. Too dangerous. There are more lucrative, *safer,* ways to serve the crown," Abel growled with a dismissive wave, "Besides, the work of a 'despised publican' is what kept a roof over your head for lo these many years," he glowered at the insult.

"There goes my holiday," Cyrano muttered.

Gassendi looked closer at Cyrano's face and continued to gape at his nose, which made him self-conscious. "Oh, dear. Well, under the circumstances, perhaps we should wait until Hercule fully recovers in a few weeks before we commence with his course of study."

"My name is Cyrano, *Monsieur*. Please call me Cyrano—wait a moment, did you say? Er, *yeess*, Father, I *am* feeling a little weak...and could use some rest here at the *château*." He quickly feigned illness by clutching the railing of the step but secretly his heart felt lighter. He tried to stifle a smile.

"Fine, fine, Hercule." Abel gave another wave. "But, in the meantime, you will apprentice with me and I will finally teach you an appreciation for the visual arts - something that will serve you well in the courts, noble *or* legal."

Cyrano's spirits clouded again. He sensed his summer fun quickly evaporating and he would have no spare time for--his friend! He almost forgot. "Father, what about Le Bret? I invited him to summer with us, starting tomorrow."

"Who? Your friend? Henri Le Bret? Well, I suppose he could *accompany* you if he is still here when you commence your studies."

Cyrano winced. Not only was he trapped in more unnecessary schooling, but now, thanks to his wrangling, he managed to jeopardize his friend's summer freedom in the process. How was he ever going to explain *that* to Le Bret?

While Cyrano wrung his hands, Abel continued to consummate the deal with Gassendi, "That alright with you, Professor? I can increase your compensation accordingly."

"Double tuition?' Gassendi whispered to himself. He cleared his throat. "Ahem, Yes, Lord Bergerac, I believe that is an agreeable arrangement." He bowed deeply, as he smiled to himself. He reached for his hat, and turned to leave.

Cyrano watched as Gassendi startled slightly as he encountered Yvette on the way out. "Oh!" was all he could muster. He looked around avoiding her gaze. Was he trying not to get caught leering at her shapely figure or fetchingly coiled locks? He smiled warmly as she dutifully opened the door to let him out into the humid air of the summer night.

Chapter 3

The next morning, the sun traced its rays across Cyrano's bedroom to his sullen, purple eyelids and woke him. His face felt much better, his spirits also improved. Soon, his best friend and school companion, Henri Le Bret, would arrive from the other side of the county. He also found himself one day closer to next week, when his favorite cousin, Roxanne, would return to *Domaine Bergerac* as she did every summer.

Cyrano walked over to the standing mirror in his room. *Ah!* The pain had subsided by a great amount, but he still looked like a losing Savàte street fighter, the swelling in his nose having only diminished a little. Oh, well, it would be a great story to tell Le Bret. *Le Bret! What time is it?* How he wished he could have a pocket watch during moments like this.

Cyrano threw on a billowy cotton shirt, pulled up a pair of knickers and high boots, and tore downstairs into the pantry, where Mother and Yvette discussed the day's menu with animation. That gave him the chance to grab some grapes and a biscuit and escape before they noticed him. He did not want to be reeled into some menial chore. Not today.

After quickly wrapping the food in his handkerchief and stuffing it into his vest pocket, he ran out of the front door of the *château* and down the dirt lane to the fence that marked the boundary of *Domaine Bergerac*. He looked back at his home. The three-story structure was not overly ostentatious for the home of a nobleman, but with a columned portico, mansard roof, tan stone masonry, a few more bedrooms than regular occupants, and several balconies in the front and back, the small mansion situated in *Mauvières* in the county known as Bergerac conveyed success. The small estate also had a barn, a stable, and watermill down by the stream that passed through the estate. Although he often longed for adventure in the big city of Paris or even in foreign lands, Cyrano truly loved the comfort of his home.

The boundary fence that was his immediate destination sat painfully close to the scene of yesterday's battle, but that's also where the main road ran past the estate.

Cyrano slowed down as he approached the infamous tree and checked with wariness for teenage highwaymen. When sure the coast indeed lay clear, he plopped on the ground under his favorite tree, retrieved breakfast from his vest, and waited for the carriage from town.

Less than twenty minutes later, a dark-brown, four-poster coach pulled by two chestnut stallions rolled into sight. *This has to be Le Bret's coach.* Cyrano squinted. The horses were in near-gallop. *That's unusual. I've never seen a coach driver go that fast before.* They were moving so swiftly, he could see the brim of the driver's dark hat bend back. At this rate, they would fly right past the estate. Cyrano got up and waved, thinking that Le Bret was asleep inside or had forgotten where *Domaine Bergerac* was.

The bearded driver did not acknowledge his frantic signal. Instead, in one swift motion, he reined in the steeds and pulled on the hand brake, bringing the coach to a sudden, skidding stop in front of the fence.

A familiar head full of unkempt black hair popped out of the cab and gave a hoot of excitement. "Oy, Fishmonger!"

Henri Le Bret, over a year older than his best friend, loved to poke fun at Cyrano's ancestry. The senior Savinien, Cyrano's grandfather, had been a fish salesman before being welcomed into the royal court.

"Oy, Manure-pusher!" Cyrano returned the poke; Le Bret's family owned several farms in Gascony. "Your own coach? Since when did you become *Cardinal*?"

Le Bret opened up the cab door. "Haha! I wanted to make a grand entrance, and with the help of my kin here, I think I did just that. Say hello to my personal chauffeur and cousin, Charles."

Cyrano then realized that the dark-attired, bearded driver was actually a young man of perhaps twenty-four years of age.

"I am *not* your personal livery, you whelp." The young man with the dashing goatee smiled. From his driving perch, he mock-bowed to Cyrano. "Charles Ogier de Batz, *Count D'Artagnan*, at your service. But you may call me D'Artagnan."

"Hercule-Savinien Cyrano de Bergerac at yours, sir," Cyrano returned the bow. "But you may call me Cyrano."

Le Bret nudged him and spoke loud enough for D'Artagnan to hear. "Yes, Cyrano, ever since Grandfather gave him a title last week, *Count D'Artagnan* here has been insufferable, but in his favor at least, he drives like a reckless lunatic—"

"And such horse skills may not be typical for a *Count*, but they will serve me well in the Brigade!" D'Artagnan threw Le Bret's leather valise down at him, knocking him to the ground.

"Ooof! No doubt, if the Musketeers will even take a pretty boy like you!" Le Bret shot back as he lay on the ground.

"The Musketeers?" Cyrano gaped at both of them.

D'Artagnan pulled his hat off, covered his heart with it, and stared into the distance with mock wistfulness. "Yes, my commission, and glory, awaits me in Paris." He flashed one last impeccable smile at the younger pair. "Cyrano, it was a pleasure to make your acquaintance. I can tell from your recent bruises that you are no stranger to adventure yourself. No doubt, your friend here will lead you on even more antics. Just don't let him eat you out of hearth and home."

Grabbing the reins, he turned to his cousin, who was pulling himself up from the ground, "Henri, enjoy your stay, but don't forget to write to Grandfather and tell him what a good sort I am for conveying you here from the other side of the county - *and* that I deserve a reward! I could use some spending money for all of the beautiful women I shall meet in Paris. Farewell!"

Le Bret and Cyrano delivered another mock bow in unison. "*Adieu, Count D'Artagnan, Adieuuuuu.*" They chuckled.

D'Artagnan wheeled the carriage around and the swift maneuver covered the boys in mud splatters. The shocked friends sputtered but fell over laughing at the speckled sight of each other.

Cyrano stared at the coach until it rumbled out of sight and sighed, "*The Musketeers*, Le Bret. The danger! The glory! Oh, how I envy him!"

"All right, enough of that. So now, where'd you get those shiners, *ami*?" Le Bret smiled at him. "I leave you for three days and already you find trouble…without me! Out with it. It's got to be a whale of a story."

"All in good time, *mon ami*, but first, we need to scheme. I must apologize to you now for my blunder, but thanks to my mishandling of Father, idle time will be in short supply this summer. Come on, race you back to the house!"

Chapter 4

The next few days were filled with eating, exploring, fishing in the creek that ran through Bergerac, and partridge hunting in the fields behind the estate. On several occasions, the boys believed they caught a glimpse of a strange creature in the forest that bordered the fields, but it always evaded their attempts to track it.

In between these adventures, Abel would wrangle the boys into his library and lecture them in the fine arts. Lord Bergerac was very proud of the two-hundred-odd volume library in his house as books and artwork represented a luxury and a sign of stature in French society. Cyrano proved to be a voracious reader but Le Bret was better at appreciating painting. Abel seemed to be gratified at both.

"Boys," Abel began as he paced on the wool rug of the library, "If you understand only one thing, it must be this: knowledge and culture are the foundations for future prosperity. By my estimation, such enlightenment gives you an advantage over at least two-thirds of the French population who cannot read. Why, just look at our former Regent! She and the rest of the de Medicis were unswerving patrons of the arts and it has yielded them immense influence throughout all of Europe."

"Is it true that King Louis was no older than we are when he took the throne?" Le Bret asked as he examined the binding of the volume that Abel handed him.

"Yes, indeed, and that is why Queen Marie de Medici was his regent and ruled in his stead until he was educated enough and wise enough to rule on his own. Speaking of 'wise', confidentially, I think it was unwise how the King treated his mother, especially since it was she who made him fit for royal duty. Exile; nasty thing," Abel seemed lost in his thoughts for a moment, but then recovered, "Anyway, 'fit for royal duty' is exactly my aim for you two vagabonds, as well. Now, that's enough for one day. Tomorrow, I will teach you all about the art of Rubens, La Tour, and Poussin."

The boys snickered at the name *Poussin* that sounded like the French word for 'baby chicken.' Abel arched a sharp eyebrow at them and the chortling ceased.

"On Thursday, I think it would be nice of you to visit your *Grandfather.* He has not seen you in over a month.*"*

There goes another day of summer fun flying away like a startled partridge.

Chapter 5

Another round of stuffy art lessons from Abel filled the next day.

Cyrano tried to smile wanly during the bluster, but he felt his chest slowly deflate. Summer was fleeing by without him. He hoped Father did not catch him staring out the window. To his surprise, Le Bret actually seemed engrossed in all of the diverse styles of artwork.

That evening after a dinner of canard and parsnips the boys retired to Cyrano's room. They lay on their backs and stared out the open window at the stars. Cyrano contemplated the composition of stars the same way he pondered clouds.

Le Bret, however, seemed to still be preoccupied with something else. "Do you think your father was right, *ami*?"

"I don't know. Wait, about what?"

"About arts being a key to success?"

"Maybe. If he means poetry or theater, then my future is full of hope. If he is referring exclusively to painting or drawing, then I am doomed to be a beggar on the streets of Paris. I can't draw my way out of a potato sack."

"I can," Le Bret shrugged.

Cyrano lifted himself up to stare at his friend. "What? Henri Le Bret, have you been holding out on me, or is that just an empty boast? "

Le Bret puffed out his chest, "I can draw anything you

want."

"Prove it! Draw me a picture of... Duc de Montmorency!"

Henri II, the Duc de Montmorency, was Cyrano's hero - a daring military man, dashing nobleman, and perhaps the greatest fencer in France, if not all of Europe. Unfortunately, he had a penchant for getting involved in countless petty duels of honor, which were now illegal. Cardinal Richelieu imprisoned him for it, but he still remained the idol of many young men like D'Artagnan and Cyrano.

After Cyrano found a piece of charcoal and parchment in his desk, Le Bret set to work, tongue sticking out of his mouth comically as he drew. A few minutes later, he proudly showed his sketch to Cyrano. He'd produced a highly detailed, perfectly scaled drawing of Montmorency engaged in a vicious duel, complete with grimacing face and sinewy arms.

"Le Bret, this is fantastic!" Cyrano beamed, "It is an uncanny resemblance; worthy of a museum. But for now, it shall grace the walls of my room. May I?"

"Sure."

Cyrano found a nail in another desk drawer and using his boot as an improvised hammer, tacked the likeness to his wall. That night, instead of gazing at the stars, he gazed at the drawing. He fell asleep dreaming of sword fights, battles, and glory.

Chapter 6

Thursday's weather proved exceptionally humid and the boys tried to slink out of *Domaine Bergerac* early for some swimming, but Abel was waiting for them downstairs.

"Boys, I admire your enthusiasm, but you needn't leave so early for *Grandfather's,"* a smile twitched under Abel's abundant mustache.

"But Father, er, *Papa,"* Cyrano widened his eyes in hopes that it made him appear innocent, "we uh…need an early start! Yes, it's such a *long* walk there," Cyrano twisted his mouth to prevent a smile from betraying his clever fib.

"Nonsense! Tarry a while, have a hearty breakfast - Yvette will make it for you-and I shall have a carriage bring you there. *Directly.*"

The boys winced. Abel thwarted their plan as deftly as an expert fencer turning aside an attack. *Parry!*

"But, *Father*…shouldn't we…wait for Roxanne to arrive? I'm sure *Grandpapa* would love to see her, too!" *Counter-Riposte!*

Abel seemed to shroud his own crafty smile beneath his burly mustache. "True enough, but I think the time is ripe for you to have a 'men-only' visit with him." *Parry and Touché!*

Cyrano slumped his shoulders, and sighed, *Se rendre.* He glanced sideways at Le Bret. "It won't be that bad, *ami,"* he whispered. "Truth be told, since *Grandfather* retired from public life, he's become somewhat entertaining. He's as crazy as a loon."

Le Bret tilted his head slowly. "Sounds like fun. What are we waiting for?"

* * * *

The carriage that conveyed them to the country home of Savinien Cyrano de Bergerac - the senior was one that Cyrano's father used for crown business. The coach was one of the perks of being a royal solicitor – one that Father usually did not abuse for personal use, but since his grandfather's simple retirement tract lay less than a league away from their own estate, Father did not see the harm in a twenty-minute trip, "just to exercise the horses," he told the boys.

Grandfather's home outside of Libourne looked too large to be considered a cottage, but it still proved modest in comparison to the grand estates of other retired *courtiers*. The home, in the fading-in-popularity Tudor style of architecture, suited the seemingly paranoid Savinien just fine; a more ostentatious and trendy domicile might draw the attention and avarice of a church inquisitor. The Church's Inquisition was centuries old and its influence was clearly waning. Nonetheless, it remained hardly toothless, and there existed no easier target for them than an old nobleman. The Inquisition might have easily stripped a Sardinian half-Jew like Savinien of his property on trumped-up charges of heresy, had he not faded into obscurity.

When they arrived by carriage, Cyrano and Le Bret found *Grandfather* in the garden behind the cottage. His hair seemed to be whiter and his beard a little longer than Cyrano remembered. He was standing on a bench, arms outstretched in a salute to the rising sun, one hand holding a saber. He needed nothing more than a barber's bowl upon his head to look like a burley French version of Don Quixote, a book that Cyrano adored.

Le Bret remained stunned at the spectacle. "What is he *doing?*" he whispered to his friend.

"Don't ask," Cyrano whispered back without taking his eyes off of the old man.

Chapter 7

"I thought you said he was a fishmonger," Le Bret whispered as the two approached the old man from behind with much caution.

"That was before he was knighted in one of the old wars," Cyrano murmured back. "He's not completely mad. It's just that…every now and then, he forgets, and he thinks that he is still a *chevalier.* That is why it is not wise to startle him. One time when I surprised him, he almost cut off my ear."

"Saints preserve!" Le Bret blessed himself with haste.

Cyrano arched an eyebrow. "Indeed. Saint Peter."

Le Bret chortled at Cyrano's irreverent reference to St. Peter's ear-cutting history, and it startled the old knight who whirled clumsily, swinging the saber around wildly and nearly falling off of his perch.

"Whoa!! *Grandpapa*! It is I…Hercule…Young Cyrano!"

When his grandmother was still living, it became confusing when she called the name Savinien, so the family took to calling him Hercule or Young Cyrano which he considered a term of great endearment and relished greatly.

"What? Oh, Ah! Young Cyrano. So glad to see you. I was just—"

"Saluting your fallen comrades, *Grandpapa.* Yes, I know." Cyrano extended a hand to help him down.

"Ah, the religious wars, Young Cyrano, they were a terrible thing." Savinien shook his head. "It really wasn't the fault of the Huguenots, you know. Tsk. Ironically, the Church doesn't take too kindly to freedom of worship. Some of my fellow noblemen wound up on the wrong side of that disagreement and were stripped of land and title. And what did the Huguenots get? Empty promises."

Sitting down on the bench to catch his breath, Savinien looked up at his grandson for a moment and smiled. "But that's nothing I probably haven't told you a dozen times before, eh? Here, let's have a look at you." He stood and considered him. "Hmmm, broken nose. Fighting again, eh? You young ones need to learn the fine art of dueling. I am too old to teach you the ways of the sword, but it is much more civilized than using your fists."

"I would love nothing more, but dueling has been outlawed, Grandpapa."

"Well, no matter." Savinien grimaced slightly at Cyrano's face. The purple bruises had started to disappear; his distended nose, not so much. "Always wear your battle scars with pride. Remember that. So, who is your friend, here?"

"Grandpapa, allow me to introduce Henri Le Bret de Mousseau; but you may call him Le Bret as you call me Cyrano."

"A pleasure, *Monsieur* Le Bret." Savinien brought the hilt of his sword to his face and gave a formal salute.

"The pleasure is all mine, *Capitaine Bergerac*." Le Bret returned the bow without a hint of disrespect.

"Grandpapa, not that I need a reason to visit, but Father said that we might have some definite purpose in seeing you today?"

"Ah, Cyrano, I have some bad news. One of your favorites, Blaise, is dead."

"No! Cyrano gasped. An aching welled up inside his chest as he recalled memories of Blaise in his grandfather's barn. "What happened?"

Le Bret looked at his friend with a knitted brow.

"Grandpapa raises and trains horses, and Blaise was one of his finest colts," Cyrano explained.

"Ahhh, I see. What a sin."

"Sin, indeed. Murder! And I want you two to help me avenge his death. Cursed wolf!" Savinien slapped his hands on his knees and pushed himself up to standing. "My boys, we are going on a hunt. I shall make great horsemen, *chevaliers,* of you, yet. A wolf has been terrorizing the local estates, eating chickens, small livestock. At first, I thought it was just a fox, but when I saw the evidence of the ruthless destruction of Blaise, I knew no fox could take down a horse. It had to be a wolf. He must be stopped. Not just to avenge the death of a horse, but because if we don't, I fear he will get bolder and his next victim will be human."

Cyrano thought about the wolf for a moment. Could that have been the strange creature he and Le Bret were ineptly trying to track in their woods? Just how large of a territorial range did wolves have? Could one lone wolf roam from the south end of Libourne to the north edge of Bergerac?

Cyrano startled out of his contemplating when Savinien raised his saber above his head and ran for the stable, yelling, "To Battle! *Vive le Fraaaaaaaaaance*!"

Cyrano turned and shrugged at his bewildered friend. "I told you he was crazy. Shall we join him?"

"Why not?"

They turned, joined in Savinien's battle-cry, and laughed as they raced after the eccentric old man.

Chapter 8

Savinien picked out two strong young stallions, *Storm,* a black Arabian, and *Demon*, a very dark chestnut Arabian, from the stable.

Since the end of the Crusades, European soldiers were enamored with the sleek, narrow-faced horses from the Turkish world. They took some home from the religious wars and for the next five-hundred years, bred them with the local stock to create the strongest, darkest, swiftest, most high-strung equines in the world. Savinien was particularly fond of the breed.

He supervised the boys in bridling and saddling them. He also issued them with pikes and muskets so they would be a fully equipped, three-person hunting party.

The old man mounted his personal horse, *Warrior*, and whirled his mount around with expertise to address the boys. "Wolves always head to high country after they make a kill, to hide out and sleep off their full bellies. My guess is, he has already found today's meal. If we hurry, we can catch up to him before sundown and before he reaches his lair."

Even Cyrano had to marvel at the skill his grandfather displayed on horseback - he proved no doddering old fool in the saddle. They headed north at a full gallop; Savinien served as the 'point' and the two boys on either 'wing.'

Under his grandfather's direction, the three crisscrossed the meadows of the estate in a meticulous hunting pattern.

The habits of his military training served him well in such a task.

After almost an hour of this procedure, the older man spotted something near the tree line that bordered the estate. "There he is, the monster! Quickly, and carefully, my young chevaliers, we must quietly surround him and cut off his escape route to the northern hills."

Savinien nudged *Warrior* and took off in pursuit, leaving the boys in a cloud of dust.

"Ack, are you still sure he is a harmless old man?" Le Bret sputtered after coughing twice.

"I can't decide who is in more danger: him, the wolf, or *us*," Cyrano responded. "Come, we'd better do as he says."

The two galloped ahead, and after a few dozen yards, broke off into a 'Y' so they could approach from opposite directions. They followed Savinien into the tree line and found him brandishing a pike above his head, ready to throw it at a dark beast that sat crouched on its haunches, ready to leap at its attacker. Its wild orange eyes menaced from the black abyss of its coat. Savinien matched the wolf's growls with his own guttural noises.

"Cyrano, my friend, I have known many loons quite saner than your grandfather!" Le Bret called.

Cyrano felt his pulse quicken and his neck flush.

Stay calm, Cyrano reminded himself while he formulated a plan. *Smarter to stay on horseback; remember how the superiority of height served you at the apple tree! Grandfather probably wants the honor of the kill, but best to end this quickly before he gets his throat ripped out!*

He reached back in the saddlebag for his short-barreled musket. He had already primed and loaded it back at the stable, and only hoped that the musket ball had not jostled out during the ride. Using his left forearm as a rest, he trained the musket on the beast.

Ker-paughh!

The muzzle blast shocked Cyrano, because it was not his own. It came from his left, a good ten yards off. Did Le Bret fire first? The wolf yelped and rolled at the feet of *Warrior.*

Savinien, Le Bret, and Cyrano all looked up to see four men on horseback. Black powder smoke surrounded all of them. In the confusion, the wolf rebounded and promptly limped off to the North.

"Ber-ger-ac, you've been warned before about poaching on my land."

The man lazily addressing Savinien wore the finery of a nobleman: embroidered jacket, brocaded vest, colorful ribbons, and leather gloves. His long, wavy locks and perfectly coiffed mustache hinted that this man let the others in his party do his dirty work, especially the one with the black leather jerkin, nasty facial scar, and smoking pistol.

"De Guiche! You know very well I am hunting a killer, not seeking sport! Look at that, he's gone now. I would have finished him for sure if you had not interfered. Now, God knows whether he is mortally wounded or just in pain and more desperate and vicious than ever." Savinien hissed at the nobleman.

"Hmm, yes. Well, nevertheless, my game warden here," De Guiche nodded to the scar-faced man, "can attest to the fact that you are on *my* hunting grounds."

Cyrano came to his grandfather's defense and steered *Storm* between him and the dandy. "What was my grandfather to do? Let a whole herd of his horses be lost to that beast?"

"And I have been losing a fair amount of my hunting dogs to that senile old coot mistaking them for 'that beast.'

Young man, may I introduce you to our constable? Perhaps we should let him settle this at the local magistrate...."

Savinien's face got even redder. "Gladly—"

"Errr, hehe, that won't be necessary," Le Bret interjected as he also positioned his horse between the antagonists. "I mean, really, *Monsieur* De Guiche—"

"*Count* De Guiche."

"Err, yes...*Count*...De Guiche. May I ask, your missing hunting dogs, you have seen no sign of them? No bodies? Really, that doesn't mean that Captain Bergerac mistook them for a wolf and slaughtered them. There would have been more evidence. A wolf would have been more likely to drag them off."

"*Count*, I am a *chevalier*." Savinien added, "If I had made such a mistake, I would have sought you out immediately and owned up to it, for the sake of my own honor. I knew from the tracks and other physical signs that I was looking for a lone wolf and not a pack. If your dogs travel together, I would have never made such an error in judgment."

Le Bret continued. "Yes...*yes*! Your hounds may have fallen victim to the same monster as his horses. So you see, Count, he may have been doing you a service as well as himself by hunting down this beast. Surely, two good neighbors can settle this amicably?"

De Guiche sneered and rolled his eyes. "Very well, but... old man, this is the last time I am going to warn you. The next time I find you on my land, perhaps my game warden shall mistake *you* for a wolf."

Cyrano noted that the fourth member of the nobleman's party was a boy about his age with the same wavy hair and sneer as the Count. Must be a De Guiche offspring.

"Thank you for your understanding, Count. We shall trouble you no further." Le Bret managed an insincere smile.

Still fiercely protective of his grandfather, Cyrano could only scowl. He never liked backing down from a fight, but he trusted his friend's judgment. He must have a reason.

"What the hell was that all about?" he asked him on the ride back to the cottage.

"Look, what is your dream? To join the Musketeers or the Gascon Guard, right? And I want to go to university."

"And your point is?"

"My point, *mon ami*, is that it's not a good idea to make too many highly placed enemies…at least, not until *after* we reach our goal. Besides, what if we went to the local magistrate and he saw what a lunatic your grandfather is? You don't want him declared insane and his estate seized by the church, do you?" He smiled a genuine smile at Cyrano. "You may have your payback someday, but all in good time."

"Le Bret, you have a shadowy scheming side I never knew about. I kind of like it! What is it you want to study at University? Politics?" Cyrano laughed.

For most of the ride home, Savinien was sullen and quiet. Finally, he spoke. "De Guiche and those men know nothing of honor. They may be noblemen, but they are far from noble. I do not want that same fate for you two. When your father's driver comes for you, I am going to send him back and have him tell your father that you will be staying on for another day. Tomorrow, your education truly begins."

"Education?" *Mon Dui!* Yet another school?

"Yes, education. A truly unique one"

Chapter 9

Dinner that night at the cottage consisted of mutton and vegetables from the farmlands. At the table, Savinien seemed sullen. He asked the boys to get up early and see to the horses, "I know that our shared wish is for a fine military career for you, but I tell you truthfully, I could use your help. Some days, just some days mind you, tending the farm *and* the horses becomes a bit much for these old bones. The events of today made me a bit weary."

"Sure, Grandpapa," Cyrano hoped that his cooperation would cheer up his grandfather. Then an idea came to him. He would share it with Le Bret tomorrow.

After breakfast the next day, the boys headed to the stable. Grandfather slept in, and they were left to their own designs, as Cyrano had hoped. He was still worried about Grandpapa's mood.

While Le Bret filled the troughs with oats, Cyrano pulled a crossbow, musket and pike off of the wall.

"Are you actually going to do something with all of that junk, or are you just trying to get me to do all of the work here?" Le Bret asked while he brushed the horses.

"We're going to hunt down that wolf ourselves and finish him off."

The boys saddled the steeds that they rode yesterday and led them quietly out of the barn.

After a short ride past the meadows, Cyrano saw something on the periphery of his vision: black, low to the ground, swift, but limping. Le Bret caught up to him and swiped at his arm. "I see it," Cyrano acknowledged, and swung *Storm* toward the shadowy beast.

The animal had to be the wolf from yesterday as it bore bloody wounds. It was clearly spooked from the noise of their approach. Cyrano hoped that the pain and fear would force the beast into a fatal mistake. He would have to make good, careful choices himself. Grandfather's words about a desperate, vicious animal still rang in his ears.

The wolf retreated into an extremely dense part of the woods, which was indeed a tactical error. The trees were so close together that they formed the wooden equivalent of a box canyon.

Cyrano pulled on the reins and veered *Storm* sideways, Le Bret did the same with *Demon*, cutting off the animal's only avenue of escape.

The boys grabbed pikes and jumped down to the floor of the forest. The wolf growled and snapped at them alternately as they came at him from forty-five degree angles.

Cyrano could clearly see his red-yellow eyes. He sensed that the creature knew that he was trapped and at the end-game. It whine-howled mournfully. A wave of pity spread over Cyrano despite the fact that on the other end of his spear was a killer.

"No," Cyrano whispered to his friend.

"What??" Le Bret was incredulous.

"This needs to be swift and as humane as possible. One musket blast and it will be over."

Le Bret scowled and huffed, "Well hurry up and get it. I'm not sure how long I can hold him."

To Cyrano's surprise, the wolf did not lunge at Le Bret or the horses. It seemed resigned to its fate. *Is it giving up, or...relieved?*

He quickly grabbed the already loaded and charged hand-musket from his saddle bag. He reminded himself of the way *Blaise* was torn apart to cement his resolve.

"Sorry," he whispered and pulled the trigger.

KER-PAUGH. The report of the hand-musket seemed to reverberate forever.

The wolf buckled immediately as the musket ball penetrated his skull, which was what Cyrano hoped for: an expeditious execution.

Almost immediately, the shouts of men and dogs came towards them. No time for remorse; time to move.

"Quickly, help me load him onto my horse!"

"Why don't we just leave him?"

"Hopefully, if we bring back proof, Grandpapa will feel avenged, or at least relieved."

In seconds, they were on their way.

When the boys returned to the stable, they found Savinien waiting for them.

Savinien examined the mound of deep onyx fur slung over Cyrano's horse and sighed in relief, "The Devil in the flesh. Well, this monster won't be haunting us any longer. Well done, boys. Dangerous, but well done."

Cyrano wondered what Grandpapa would say if he knew that he had sympathy for the devil.

Savinien scrutinized the boys and the carcass of the wolf again, "Bravery, honor, and even ingenuity. Yes, I am sure of it now. You boys are ready. Ready for a new kind of knowledge."

Dinner that night was a simple but savory chicken and mushroom stew. Grandfather was still uncharacteristically quiet during the meal, but something was different this time. It didn't seem like he was still nursing his wounded pride from the encounter with De Guiche. Instead, he wore a wry smile. Despite urging from Cyrano, he gave no further hints or details of the 'knowledge' he had in mind for the boys.

Finally, as the shadows of the day grew longer, he solemnly addressed them. "We are going into town. You don't have the proper clothes with you, so I am going to lend you two of my dark jackets."

As dusk approached, they mounted their horses again and Savinien led them to Bordeaux, the largest town closest to Bergerac. On the outskirts of town, they came upon a well-crafted stone building that looked like a church but had no cross on it.

Savinien dismounted and the boys followed suit. They were intrigued, but dared not ask any questions.

The old man took something that looked like a rolled-up dark cloth out of his saddle pouch. "You will see things in here, secret things. If you agree to enter, you must never speak of them to anyone."

Cyrano felt flutters in the center of his gut. Grandfather had never been so enigmatic before, but he still trusted him un-waveringly. "Not even Father?" He could not disguise the shock in his voice.

Savinien smiled. "Abel knows already; has he ever mentioned this place to you?"

Cyrano shook his head.

"Good. He's not supposed to. Hopefully, you can be as good a secret-keeper as the rest of the Bergerac clan."

As they entered the anteroom of the building, Savinien unraveled the cloth and wrapped it around himself. A black apron with odd markings. How strange.

He led them to a closed set of tall double doors. Muffled talking sounded from behind it. Savinien cleared his throat loudly. Suddenly, three knocks came at the door. Savinien returned three knocks as well and the panels opened.

They entered a large room lit by many candles. The silhouettes of many men peopled the chamber, their faces obscured by darkness. A tall, shadowy figure, also wearing an apron, stood at a podium at the front of the room. He addressed Cyrano's grandfather. "Brother Warden, are these that enter Apprentice Masons from the West?"

"They are, your Worshipfulness," Savinien replied.

"Who presents these candidates?"

"A Master Mason, armed with the proper implements of his office," Savinien responded.

"Very well. As there are no other candidates from the North, South, or East, I now declare this Lodge of Free Masons of the Knights Templar, the Knights of the Red Cross, and the Knights of the Hospitallers, open."

Cyrano and Le Bret took their cues from Savinien and tried to keep with the serious decorum of the meeting by staying quiet and standing stiffly at attention like soldiers. However, they struggled not to gape at all of the strange trappings and ciphers all over the room.

The pomp, waving of symbolic objects, and ritualized movements lasted for a good fifteen minutes until finally the man at the podium, the one called the Master of the Lodge, addressed Cyrano's grandfather again.

"Brother Warden, you will take the candidates, and Brother Senior will help you with their lessons."

Cyrano could see Le Bret visible tense up as they were led to yet another strange dark, room— this one even darker and more peculiar than the last, but Cyrano maintained his supreme trust in his grandfather.

Savinien instructed the boys to sit down at a bench. "It is a great honor that the Lodge Master bestowed upon us. Most candidates are blindfolded, but he knows you are in our care and are trustworthy with the ancient secrets."

The one called Brother Senior came closer and spoke to them in hushed tones.

"Hundreds of years ago, the Templar Knights were the main army, bank, and police force of the Christian world. These were duties that the knights took very seriously. After all, they had to protect women, children, the elderly, and pilgrims as they traveled back and forth across many lands. People trusted them. Therefore, they felt that they had to be of the highest moral character or they would shame themselves and their order."

Savinien continued in the same quiet voice. "The Templars were betrayed by a greedy king and nearly wiped out. Some escaped and went into hiding. In order to survive, they taught themselves how to be stone masons, but they never forgot their vows of Chivalry. They continued to meet in secret and used the tools of the mason as symbols of their continued faith in the Knights' Code of Conduct."

Brother Senior pulled out three objects from a velour sack and put them on a table in front of the boys. "The Level is a symbol of Equality. All men are equal—no one is better than another, even if they are of noble birth. The Square is a symbol of morality. Just like a square is used for measuring, you should compare your actions to what is morally right. The Plumb is a symbol of straightness. To be a knight, your path in life must be straight and righteous. Do you think that you could commit to such a path?"

Cyrano and Le Bret instinctively nodded but dared not say a word.

Savinien sat on the bench next to the boys and lowered his voice to a complete whisper for dramatic effect. "Here is the Code that a truly honorable knight lives by: have faith and hope; protect the weak and defenseless; comfort the poor; refrain from drunkenness; never expect reward; serve your country with bravery and valor; obey the law, unless the law hurts the defenseless."

Brother Senior continued. "Guard the honor of fellow knights; avoid cheating; pledge loyalty to your family; at all times, speak the truth; always finish what you start; respect the honor of women; never refuse a challenge from an equal; and never, ever abandon or turn your back on anyone, even a foe."

"Remember these things, especially when you encounter dishonorable men like De Guiche," Savinien added. "Can you swear your allegiance to the Code and the honorable life of a Knight?"

Cyrano looked over at Le Bret in the shadows. He was not sure how his friend was receiving this message, but as for himself, he felt that every one of the codes rang true and burned into his very soul. *This is true. This is right. This is the only way to live a worthy life.*

"Yes." Cyrano was shocked to hear that Le Bret committed to the same oath as he almost simultaneously.

"Good," Savinien nodded slowly, "Because you have made such a commitment tonight, you have opened many doors. Behind many of those doors lie secrets and knowledge lost to the outside world. Within the libraries of Freemasonry lies a fortune in books and manuscripts filled with ideas and plans for machines, tools, and weapons even more wondrous than you with your exceptional mind could imagine. Someday, you may prove yourself worthy of that information."

Brother Senior gave a satisfied look at Savinien. "I think that is enough for tonight. They have a lot to remember and think about."

On the way home, even in the dark, Cyrano recognized the road and became concerned. *"Grandpapa,* I think we took a wrong turn. This is not the way back to your farm."

"I know. I am taking you back to *Domaine Bergerac*."

"But…but *Grandpapa*, how can you manage to take three horses back to your home in the dead of night?"

"I won't have to. I am making a gift of *Storm* and *Demon* to you and Le Bret."

The boys practically jumping out of their saddles. "Thank you! Thank you! Oh, we will take such good care of them, we swear!"

Savinien stopped *Warrior* for a moment to give Cyrano a smile. "Everything comes back to trust. Can you imagine what an honor it was for a Christian order such as we saw tonight to initiate a half-Jew like me? I vowed never to betray that trust. Now, I show you that same level of trust. This has been a long time coming, Cyrano. You are a good grandson, and I see what a good, honorable man you are becoming, and I also see that you choose your friends wisely. Besides, what is a *chevalier* without a horse?"

Chapter 10

The next morning, *Domaine Bergerac* teemed with activity and anticipation. Roxanne was due to arrive for her annual summer stay. She was Cyrano's favorite relative although the relationship was fairly distant, akin to third cousins. When they were younger, they would run around the estate, throw stones in the river, laugh, fight, make up, trade secrets, and share dreams.

Cyrano had not seen her in almost a year. A lot of growing up can happen in that much time. In light of last night's event, he felt he had personally matured quite a bit. How much had Roxanne changed? In some ways, he looked forward to finding out, but in other ways, he also dreaded it. *Suppose she is taller than me, or acts all sophisticated?* Cyrano had a plan, just in case.

When mid-day arrived, Cyrano and Le Bret decided to greet Roxanne's carriage on horseback. They looked at each other smugly as if to say, "Look at us, big deals with our sleek, new stallions, eh?"

Finally, Roxanne's carriage pulled up to the fence at the edge of the estate. The door of the carriage opened up and a stunningly beautiful young lady emerged in a dress that must be at the height of fashion in Paris and the same color as the summer sun. Cyrano gulped audibly when he saw her. Her yellow dress complimented her long, strawberry blonde tresses, which were not pinned up the way most girls her age wore. Instead, they fell around her, highlighting a classically shaped neck and shoulders. If he stared at her electric-blue eyes for too long, he would have missed out on the few freckles that dotted her cheeks and the bridge of her nose. It was rumored by their relatives that somewhere back in time, Roxanne's branch of the family tree had mingled with Irish folk which would explain the fair skin, the sprinkling of freckles, and red-tinged locks that made her look like a cross between an angel and a wood nymph.

Cyrano gasped. Sacrebleu! *She has changed!*

The vision in yellow put her hands on her hips and smiled up at him mischievously. "Well, how in the hell am I supposed to hug you while you are up on that long-necked donkey?"

Thank God. Still salty. She hasn't changed that much! Cyrano sighed and smiled, "Henri Le Bret, allow me to introduce Madeleine de Robineau, but she is affectionately known to the family as Roxanne. And Roxanne, dear cousin, this is my good friend, Le Bret."

"Ah, so this is your partner in crime you were talking about last summer! *Salut*, Le Bret!"

Before Le Bret could clear his throat and deliver a gallant greeting, Roxanne threw her travel bag at him and clambered up on top of Cyrano's horse, "Ooof! Why are people always throwing luggage at me?" he complained.

"Well, let's get going, cousin! Summer won't last forever. We have lots of plans to make; and stop trying to impress your friend over there with your manners. This is me you are talking to."

Roxanne wrapped her arms around Cyrano's waist. His heart skipped several beats and flushed his ears with blood as he felt the warmth of her hands on him. Feeling his cheeks getting redder, he shot a goofy smile at Le Bret and spurred

Storm back to *Domaine Bergerac*.

Chapter 11

The three were on their best behavior at the lunch table under Mother's, and Yvette's, watchful eyes. But after the meal and after they had helped to clear the table, they scrambled upstairs to Cyrano's room.

"So, have you had any chance to go exploring yet?" Roxanne asked with excitement thrumming in her lilting voice.

Cyrano remembered what she was referring to and shook his head. "Not exactly. We went hunting in the woods, but only for partridge, not for ghosts. We didn't venture in too deeply."

"I'm telling you, Cyrano, those woods on the edge of the estate are haunted!"

Le Bret raised an eyebrow. "Spirits? And you are not afraid?"

Roxanne cast a withering look his way.

Cyrano'd better run interference before a spat broke out. "Cousin, it is so good to have you back here. Remember when we were younger? We would go down to the river, and I would fence with a river-reed and you would pretend to heal my wounds?"

He wanted no tension in the house for this visit. He recognized his own stubbornness, and Roxanne was nearly his equal—one of many reasons he'd grown so fond of her. She was smart, cultured, adventurous, and willful, just like him.

In their younger days, he would practically forget that she was a girl. With her now-blossoming beauty, he could no longer ignore the fact that his fondness was growing into something deeper. *I wonder what she thinks of me....* He was grateful that she said nothing about his broken nose. *Was she being polite? Doubtful; that is not her way. Am I just invisible to her? Or, dare I hope that she thinks my face now makes me look dangerous?*

"Why didn't you tell me the woods were haunted, and why didn't we check it out for ourselves last week? Remember the odd thing we thought we saw?" Le Bret was undaunted by the change of subject.

"Because they *aren't* haunted. The peculiar thing we saw was probably the wolf," Cyrano threw back with impatience. "And...I promised Roxanne I would wait for her return before we explored." He shrugged.

"Ah, but Cousin, they *are* haunted, and we are going to find a real-live ghost."

"That's absurd. I am a man of science and besides, by definition, any spirit we would find there would not be 'live'," Cyrano concluded.

"But all scientists have one thing in common, my love, and that is an incurable curiosity!"

Did she just say 'my love'? Agree to whatever she says, you imbecile! "Oh, very well, but if we are going to find one, it obviously has to be at night. Mother and Father sleep like the dead, but getting past Yvette will be tricky, indeed."

"Then it's settled. Tonight, we rest well because tomorrow, we will sneak out of the house when it is good and dark, say ten o'clock?" Roxanne directed with a firm tone.

Le Bret rolled his eyes. "Why not just make it the witching hour? Perhaps there are witches out there, too."

"Very well, then, let's make it midnight." Roxanne accepted the challenge.

They returned downstairs to the parlor to play a game of Charades, but the real charade was yet to come and would be for the benefit of Cyrano's parents. At nine o'clock, the sky had turned dark and they innocently feigned sleepiness, in order to establish a pattern for tomorrow night. Before they retired to their respective rooms, Mother stopped them all. "Hercule...."

Cyrano gritted his teeth. Why couldn't the rest of his family address him as Cyrano, the same way Grandfather and Roxanne did? "Yes, Mother?"

"I was thinking...."

Uh-oh....

"I was thinking, now that your cousin is here, why don't you three visit Aunt Marie tomorrow? Your godmother adores you both so much."

Cyrano and Roxanne sighed and looked at each other. He could read the dejection on her face. Not that they didn't love Marie Feydau; she doted over them and shared her wisdom and her boundless supply of pastries and treats. It was just that, well, it was *summer.* Suddenly, Roxanne's face brightened.

"One moment, cousin Esperance," Roxanne smiled at his mother, while she pulled him out of the room.

"Huh?"

"It won't be that bad," Roxanne whispered as she patted his arm.

"How do you figure that?" he whispered back.

"She is very learned and newsy, to boot. Perhaps she has some clues about The Ghost of Gascony Forest."

Cyrano could not help but snicker. "Oh, so now your fictitious ghost has a name as well as an imaginary legend?"

"Why, we would love to visit Aunt Marie!" Roxanne

addressed her aunt out loud as they returned to the room. She continued to smile at her even while she sung under her breath to Cyrano. "You're going to regret mock-ing meeee!"

Chapter 12

"Aunt" Marie Feydau was one of Abel and Esperance de Bergerac's oldest friends, but not a relative at all. Born into a simple family, her husband didn't care about her breeding, only her exceptional beauty, and her life took a dramatic turn when they married. As the wife of a nobleman, she became much better educated than the typical 17th century French woman. Formal education for women, beyond a convent school, proved rare. However, her husband insisted that his wife needed to be more than a trophy wife and had to hold her own in all kinds of conversations while entertaining other members of the royal court. Therefore, he imported tutors to come to their estate and educate her.

Marie took to the lessons eagerly, and her wit, spirit, and charm made her an instant hit among the courtiers. Her naturally platinum-blonde hair meant that she did not have to wear a wig to gain attention, as the other noble ladies resorted to doing, and made her as memorable as her simple charisma.

When her husband passed away, she retired from the social scene but her love for learning remained unquenchable. Unable to have children of her own, she made it her personal quest to pass on her knowledge to the offspring of her friends, none more so than Cyrano and Roxanne.

When Cyrano, Roxanne, and Le Bret arrived, Marie had plenty of cakes and treats ready. The typical routine for a visit included eating, discussions about literature, eating, poetry reading, and, oh yes, lots of eating.

Le Bret tried to be politely attentive, but he was far more interested in drawing than in the poetry being discussed, and he became far more intent upon a strawberry trifle that he was cramming into his mouth than anything else.

"…But dear Roxanne, there *are* opportunities for women in the arts," Marie explained while trying to ignore Le Bret licking his fingers. "For example, Louise Labe. Her work is generations old and she is highly regarded in the world of poetry. Listen to this….

I live,
I die,
I burn,
I drown
I endure at once chill and cold
Life is at once too soft and too hard
I have sore troubles mingled with joys"

"That was written by a woman?" Roxanne brightened. She always searched for validation for her gender.

"But, of course, my dear." Marie smiled. "Who else but a woman could depict the duality of life, the conflict of love?"

"Ah, yes, pleasure and pain at the same time. How romantic!" Roxanne sighed.

To Cyrano, it felt as though he watched a slow tennis match, trying to follow the ladies' conversation while still taking in the abomination of Le Bret's bingeing. Marie glanced over at him.

"Poetry is not just for the fair gender, Cyrano. There are plenty of epic poems filled with excitement for adventure seekers like you. Consider *The Song of Roland*:

Count Roland sprang to a hill - top's height, And donned

his peerless armor bright; Laced his helm, for a baron made; Girt Durindana, gold - hilted blade; Around his neck he hung the shield, With flowers emblazoned was the field; Nor steed but Veillantif will ride; And he grasped his lance with its pennon's pride. White was the pennon, with rim of gold; Low to the handle the fringes rolled. Who are his lovers men now may see; And the Franks exclaim, 'We will follow thee.

It gets even more thrilling than that later."

"Really? With blood and gore, and all that?" Cyrano perked up.

"Ha, well, sort of. It is certainly a ballad about the glory of knighthood, but I'm not going to recite the entire epic for you. If you want to know how it turns out, you shall have to read it for yourself. Here." Marie handed him a volume from a nearby shelf.

Knighthood. Cyrano rubbed his chin as he recalled the night with the Masons.

Aunt Marie smiled. Did she know that Cyrano was intrigued? Is that what she had hoped?

She turned her attention to the display of gluttony behind them. "And what of you, Monsieur Le Bret? Any style of verse that you are partial to?"

He shook his head. "Murffee. I mean, *merci*," He managed to get out a muffled but polite decline out of his éclair-stuffed mouth.

"Aunt Marie, you know so much about literature. Do you know of any books about ghosts?" Roxanne tried, without success, to make it sound nonchalant and not like an interrogation.

Cyrano recovered his tea saucer with a clatter. He did not expect his cousin to be so blunt.

Marie laughed. "Well, my dear, I'm afraid things such as ghosts are more the subject of folk tales than books."

"You have lived in Gascony your whole life. Have you ever heard stories of any ghosts in this area?" Roxanne moved to the edge of her seat in anticipation.

Marie gave her a sweet smile. "Roxanne, every town in France, and perhaps every village in Europe, has their share of myths, whether it's ghosts, devils, or angels walking the earth. Why, I've even heard folk stories that in Carpathia, there are monstrous men that drink the blood of other men. *Vampeers*, I think they call them. Tsk-tsk. Ridiculous. Anyway, I prefer to ponder the qualities of love over mysticism." She must have read the dejection in the young girl's face, and added, "But far be it from me to snuff your youthful zeal. You never know what you will find unless you seek it."

Later, as they walked out to the horses, Cyrano gave voice to his dismay. "Roxanne, why do you persist in this silly crusade for a ghost?"

She whirled at him. "Don't you understand? If I actually see a ghost, I could write about it." She gasped. "Oh, Cyrano! What if we encounter a *vampeer*? What a book that would make! It could launch me on a career as an author or poet."

"We'd be famous," Cyrano reasoned aloud, "They'd *have* to accept me in the Musketeers if I captured a blood-sucking devil!"

"Oh, dear cousin, I don't want to do it to be famous. I just don't want to be useless. I don't want to be a nun, a wife, or, heaven forbid, just languishing in the royal court!"

"Well, better to be a court-ier than to be a *court-esan…*," he replied with a devious grin.

Roxanne scowled. "And *you* should be a *court-jester*, you wicked imp! Courtesan indeed! Being some fat, old nobleman's secret plaything is the worst fate I could possibly imagine."

She wound up and pummeled his arm for his bawdy suggestion.

"Ow! I am already regretting mocking you." Cyrano rubbed his upper arm. "All right, if it means that much to you, we shall search the woods tonight for your poltergeist. Or *vampeer*!"

"*Au revoir*, Madame Marie, *au revoir!*" Loaded down with yet more sweets, Le Bret stumbled out of the door backwards and joined his friends.

Cyrano folded his arms. "Are you sure you would not like a grist wagon for your plunder?"

"Is there one handy?" Le Bret replied half-earnestly.

"May I?" Roxanne mock-pleaded to Cyrano.

"By all means, cousin."

Cyrano bowed out of the way as Roxanne wound up even harder and slapped Le Bret's arm.

Chapter 13

The next day proved uncommonly hot, which made for a good excuse for not doing much and resting so that they could stay awake for their midnight ghost-hunting.

That evening, once again, they feigned sleepiness, this time at around half past ten, and retired upstairs. Luckily for their plan, Abel, Esperance, and Yvette followed suit soon after.

They patiently waited an hour in the dark of their rooms until reasonably assured that the rest of the house had fallen asleep. Then with a pre-arranged knock as a cue, they crept downstairs and out the scullery door of the kitchen, feeling their way through the dark.

Once they were sure they'd reached beyond the view of the *château*, they lit the candles and lantern they had brought with them.

"Do you think it's about midnight?" Roxanne asked anxiously.

"Oh wait, let me consult my pocket watch. What do I look like, some rich Bavarian king or something?" Le Bret quipped sardonically.

Cyrano gestured skyward with his lantern. "The moon looks to be at its zenith, if that helps. I was so concerned about escaping the house quietly that I didn't listen for the hall clock or even the hourly church chimes. We are so far away from town out here that you really have to strain to hear them. And by the way, I hear that the price of watches have been coming down."

"Hmmm," Le Bret said. "One would come in handy when we go away to school. They're pretty cranky about being prompt at university. We should ask our families for going-away presents."

As they reached the tree line of the woods, Roxanne looked around nervously. "Yes, well, in we go…I guess…."

They spent the better part of an hour chasing shadows, noises, and hunches, all the while scaring each other intentionally and unintentionally until they grew beyond tired. On more than one instance, Roxanne and Cyrano bumped into each other in the dark, they laughed nervously as they brushed against each other in a lingering fashion. Finally, Roxanne announced, "Well, I hate to admit defeat, but I am tired and I don't want to get caught and snitched on by your maid. So one more sweep of one hundred paces, each of us in different directions. If we don't find anything immediately, we rendezvous back here and try another night." The boys let out grateful sighs.

"Agreed." Cyrano nodded. "Just don't get lost, or out of earshot of each other if we have to call for help."

Fatigued from all of the sugar he had eaten that day at Marie Faydeau's, Le Bret was too tired to do anything but agree as well and stumble off.

Cyrano began pacing off steps and thinking to himself, gratified that he had humored Roxanne's whim tonight. She seemed appreciative of his efforts and there also came the added bonus of being achingly close to her for most of the night; sharing a candle, whispering in each other's ear, and the touching. One time, when Roxanne thought she sensed danger, she hugged him. It became almost too much for him to bear. Even with his damaged nose, he could feel her breath, smell her hair, which through some strange Parisian craft, had the scent of gardenias. At the witching hour, he was being bewitched by Roxanne's essence.

Jolted from his reverie, he froze as he saw a very real shadow of a person not twenty paces in front of him, outlined in the moonlight. It was too tall to be Roxanne or Le Bret, and this person was clearly trying *not* to be seen. A cold feeling ran up his back. A *vampeer*?

Cyrano's mind raced, but he forced down the fear with logic. This silhouette was obviously not a ghost but a much more credible threat. *Stop thinking about blood-suckers, and more about fending off a robber.* He did not grow scared for himself; recent events proved he could handle himself if attacked. He was much more concerned about protecting Roxanne.

Finally, his mind came upon a defense. If this man was trying not to be seen, the last thing he wanted would be for someone or some event to announce his presence. Therefore, this man would not kidnap Roxanne unless he felt threatened himself. Cyrano needed to get his 'search party' out of here, and quickly. He also needed to pretend that he did not notice the man. This would nullify the tactical advantage of surprise should he be wrong and the man did attack.

"I don't see anything. How about you two?" Cyrano almost yelled this in hopes of convincing the…man (?)…that he should remain still and hidden.

"No, nothing here…." Le Bret reported back.

"Let's go home…." Roxanne sighed.

Cyrano sighed, too, but in relief. "C'mon. Let's get out of here."

"Hey! What's your hurry? You act as if you've seen…a bear." Cyrano reckoned that Roxanne resisted the temptation to say, "ghost."

"It's just that, well, the longer we stay out here, the better our chances are of getting caught by that nitwit Yvette. Do you want my father's wrath upon you for this exploit? He might send you home before summer's end."

"Ah, good point." Le Bret nodded.

Cyrano bustled them back to the *château*, all the while looking back at the woods.

Who was *that? Why did he hide?*

Cyrano's curiosity burned. Could this shadowy man have been the 'animal' he and Le Bret tried to track earlier this summer? What was he doing out there? Could he be just a beggar, or something more desperate and dangerous than the wolf they hunted? He would make it a point to find an opportunity to go back to that same spot in the woods, by himself. It would have to be some morning when the others were occupied, and find out who this uninvited guest of Domain Bergerac was. The next time, he would be prepared.

Chapter 14

After they returned home and to their respective bed-rooms, they slept off the excitement of their escapade.

Later that morning, Cyrano awoke first. Obsessed with what he saw in the woods last night, he did not sleep well.

Several things he was pretty sure of: One- that if the mysterious man was hiding out in the woods instead of a house, he was either a refugee, a runaway slave, or an es-caped convict. In any case, Cyrano was intrigued by the adventure it promised. Two- if any of the above scenarios proved true, then the man would be hungry; very hungry. Using food to draw him out might be a good strategy. Three-just in case, he should bring a weapon.

Now, to distract the others. He tried to formulate a plan that would keep them sufficiently busy this morning while he stole away.

Suddenly, he had it.

He wrapped a blanket around himself and called Le Bret and Roxanne to his room. He screwed a pained expression onto his face and pretended to shiver.

"*Mon Dieu*, you look like death! What is wrong with you?" Le Bret gasped.

"I fear I caught a chill in the night air last evening. I *feel* like death. And I fear that if I show myself to Mother or that imbecile Yvette, they will figure out that we left the house last night and our goose will be cooked."

"Oh dear, my poor cousin. It is all my fault! If it was not for my childish curiosity, you would not have fallen ill like this." Roxanne tsked and petted Cyrano's head. He nearly swooned from her touch. If this kept up, he would not have to feign dizziness.

"Oh...." He shivered from the delight of her touch, but covered it up with his feigned infirmity. Extra attention from Roxanne turned into an unexpected fringe benefit of his plan.

"Ach! What shall we do?" Le Bret wrung his hands.

"Here, I have a few coins. Take them and go into town to the apothecary...both of you...ask him for a cold remedy. I am sure that is all that I have and I will be right in a day, but we cannot let the others know."

"Good idea!" Le Bret jumped up.

"Take care, my dear, brave Cyrano!" Roxanne caressed his face.

His toes wiggled at her touch. Fortunately, they were under the blanket.

Did she see my reaction? Oh, I am a natural at this acting thing! I really must explore drama lessons when I go to university. It certainly has its rewards! Cyrano congratulated his own cleverness.

Chapter 15

With his friends safely off to town, Cyrano crept downstairs, eluded Yvette, and swiped some food. He then skulked out the pantry door undetected and made his way to his horse in the stables.

After a swift ten-minute ride, Cyrano dismounted *Storm* and left him several yards away from the edge of the woods. He wanted to have a quick means of escape, if necessary, but he didn't want to risk having his horse stolen by the mystery man, either. He pushed down the creeping, silly notion that there actually might be a *vampeer* in there waiting for him.

Don't be ridiculous. Besides, Templar Knights are brave in the face of danger, he told himself.

He entered the woods at the place he thought he saw his quarry last night. Even in the bright morning sun, the thick trees darkened the forest floor. *Our mystery man could not have picked a more perfect hiding place.*

Not knowing what else to do to draw the man out of hiding, he started to call out.

"I know you are here. I saw you last night. Don't be alarmed. I won't hurt you, but you have to show yourself. If you don't show yourself, my friends may tell the constable or the game warden that we saw *something* out here. But if you come out, I will swear them to secrecy. Look, I have food. If I meant you harm, I would not have brought you food."

He thought he heard some underbrush rustling about twenty yards ahead of him. That encouraged him.

"Look, I have fresh biscuits…and clean water…and mutton…and flint for a fire to heat it up."

He heard a low, soft, whispered curse. Cyrano was sure he was getting to him, breaking down his resistance. *Ah, can't resist the offer of fresh food, can you?*

Finally, a quiet response came in broken French. "Any butter for those biscuits?"

A chill went down Cyrano's back. *Was it fear, excitement, or a little of both.* "A bit…" he responded as he instinctively reached for the hilt of the *épée* he brought for protection. "…You aren't French, are you?"

When he heard another muffled curse, he drew his sword.

"No, I am not."

"I surmise that you are not a hermit or vagabond, either, because you conceal yourself. Yet, you are not a common thief or murderer or you would have killed my friends and I last night without a second thought. However, you *do* fear being discovered. Why so?" Cyrano felt some of his typical boldness return to him.

"You are clever, indeed. I have eluded men twice your age for a very long time."

Cyrano started to recognize the thick accent and came to a shocking realization. "You are a Spaniard?"

Silence. He had hit home. Then the rustling of the brush moved away from him.

"Wait! Don't run! I am a very loyal Frenchman, it is true, but I will not turn you in. Why would I? Our countries are no longer enemies, my friend."

The war of Mantuan Succession between France and Spain had been over for years. The year was 1633 and war officially ended in 1631.

A figure emerged from the shadows. He was somewhat gaunt, bearded, shabby, and dirty, with a pronounced limp. Even through the beard and the dark of the forest, Cyrano could see that the man was not that old, perhaps thirty. He just looked like he had been through hell, which made him look older.

He put down the sack of food in front of the man and backed away.

The grubby man descended upon the biscuits, tearing at them ravenously. He grunted as he ate. Sometimes large crumbs of bread fell into his lap and he methodically retrieved them and shoved them back into his mouth. His wildness reminded Cyrano of the wolf he hunted just a few days ago. Unlike the *lupe,* he felt great pity for this man driven to such animal-like state.

"Thank you!" The man sobbed in his Spanish-accent-laden French. "I was getting so tired of apples, berries, and grubs. That is what they teach you to survive on in the infantry."

Cyrano could now see that his shabby clothes were the remnants of a Spanish army uniform.

"Allow me to introduce myself. I am Cyrano de Bergerac." He bowed formally. "These woods are part of my family homestead. It is true that you do owe me a debt for my generosity, and this is all I ask in return: tell me your story. How did you end up here?"

The man nodded as he continued to gorge on the food.

"As I said, I am…I *was*…in the infantry. My corps had penetrated deep into enemy…French…territory, south of here. I saw many evil things in battle. Many innocents harmed or killed. I no longer believed in the righteousness of war. One day, I just left my post in disgust. My comrades all went home. I could not. I have been living in these woods ever since. I was grateful for the mild winter last year. Year... Hah, I have lost track of time." He choked on a pathetic, mournful laugh.

"But the war is over. Why are you still hiding?"

The Spaniard shook his head. "For one so clever, you are still so naïve. I cannot go home. Even though the war is over, I would be hanged as a deserter if I came limping back to Madrid in this tattered uniform. And even though our two countries are no longer at war, Spaniards aren't exactly welcome by the typical Frenchman."

Cyrano nodded grimly. He had overheard his father reading the news just last winter when the nearby townsfolk had set an entire field on fire because they thought a Spanish deserter hid in it.

"I am a man with no country. No home." The hairy man sniffed as he got up and limped around.

"How did you get that limp?" Cyrano meant the question to be sympathetic and not accusatory.

"The same way I surmise that you got your nose. It is a battle scar."

"Indeed." He laughed. "I do not know what else to say, Spaniard, other than this–by my grandfather, I have sworn allegiance to the ancient code of chivalry. I cannot turn my back on you and your plight. I am now responsible for your life. You are on my family's land, and thus, you are under my protection. As long as you want to, you can remain hidden here."

The man started sobbing again. "Thank you. I know the code, too. That is why I do not harm others who venture into these woods despite the desperation of my situation. I wish only to exist in peace. However, because I am also hon-or-bound, I am obliged somehow to repay your generosity."

"How do you propose to do that?"

"Do you know you are holding that *épée* all wrong?"

"Err...."

"I see a little of my youth in you, my friend. Do you long to be a good swordsman someday?"

"Yes, yes, indeed." Cyrano could not hide his desire.

"Well, this is what I propose–if you bring me a little morsel of food each day, I shall teach you how to be the greatest fencer of your generation. Before our two countries went to war, my dear friend, De Montmorency, was my dueling partner."

"Did you say that you knew the great Duc de Montmorency?"

Cyrano calculated all of the factors in his head. Father did not condone martial skills, so he would never pay for fencing lessons Cyrano so desperately wanted. Despite being a former chevalièr, Grandfather was too old to pass on this knowledge to him. This grungy Spaniard had no way of proving that he was the great fighter he claimed to be, or if he even met de Montmorency. However, even a little new knowledge might help. This could be his opportunity to improve his chances of getting into the Musketeers. He had no idea how he was going to steal food for his new tutor or how he was going to keep this secret from his friends. It would be risky, and that is why he liked it.

"Spaniard, you have a pact. Now, I must return home before my friends and family become suspicious. But I will be back tomorrow for my first lesson."

"*Adios*, young warrior, and many blessings on you."

Chapter 16

As he returned to the main house, Cyrano cursed his bad timing. He could see Le Bret and Roxanne returning from town up the main road at the front of the house. Unfortunately, he could also see Yvette dawdling over some menial scullery task by the back door. *Mon Dieu,* both entrances to the house thwarted.

Suddenly, he thought of a plan. It reminded him of the stories of the siege of ancient castles he so enjoyed reading thanks to Father. He looked up at the balcony of his bedroom. *Yes!* He had left the window wide open. He would have to act fast and his aim would have to be perfect.

He positioned himself in some bushes near the back of the house close to Yvette. When he found a few acorns, he hurled them at the woodpile on the far side of the house. Yvette startled and, as Cyrano hoped, the nosy girl would not resist the temptation to investigate.

It's a good thing it was just me and not a murderous gypsy, you simpleton, Cyrano mused as he sprinted under his balcony at the near side of the house.

Once again using the climbing skills he had honed on the local trees, he hoisted himself up the downspout, shimmied up to his balcony, and through his bedroom window. *Success!*

A few moments later, he heard Le Bret and Roxanne bound up the steps to his room as he kicked off his riding boots and dove for the covers.

"Cyrano! We have a powder from the apothecary." Le Bret burst into the room.

"Thank God, I thought he was going to send you back with leeches or something! I'm feeling better already."

"Really?" Roxanne examined him as she drew closer. "Because you look rather flushed…" She put a hand to his head, "…And you are sweating!"

"What? Oh, it's really nothing. I'm fine. Look, I will make a draught from that concoction the druggist gave you and I'll be as right as rain by dinner."

Cyrano tried to compose himself from his wall-scaling antics so as not to draw any more suspicion. He changed the subject in order to break their fish-eye stares. "Speaking of dinner, er lunch, I thought I heard Mother say she was going to have Yvette make blueberry tarts for dessert. Isn't that your favorite, cousin?"

Roxanne looked at him bewildered. "Er, well, sort of…."

"Yes, well, perhaps we should let your cousin rest some more. He talks like that when he gets over-tired, heh-heh. Cyrano, wouldn't you like to sleep a bit more before lunch?" Le Bret nudged his comrade.

"Er, yes. Yes! I mean, uh, I am a bit weary from fighting off this infirmity. See you all in an hour in the dining room?"

Le Bret bustled Roxanne out of the room, but before he left, he gave his friend an arched eyebrow that Cyrano understood to mean that he would be back soon, expecting an explanation.

Chapter 17

At lunch, Cyrano found himself full of regrets. Remorseful for lying to his friends, he wasn't sure how long he could keep up the ruse. Furthermore, feigning illness had its drawbacks, too. He really wanted to resume his summer fun after lunch – swimming, fishing, or *anything* outside, but a too-miraculous recovery would only invite more suspicion his way. Should he confide in his friends? Would they be angry at him for his deception? He didn't know what to do. He was miserable as he poked at his food.

"Something wrong, *chéri?*"

Mother had noticed his atypical gloominess and it startled him out of his thoughts. "Huh?"

"Don't you feel well?"

Think quick!

"Ah, er, well, actually, I was feeling…strange…this morning, but…I'm feeling much better, now."

She planted a palm on his forehead. "Hmmm, well, you are not running a fever. You say you feel better?"

"Er, yes. Pretty much so."

"Well, perhaps you need some fresh air. Why don't you all go out and commune with nature? It might do you a world of good."

"Out? Yes, ma'am!"

Cyrano scrambled from the table and headed for the door.

His shocked friends must instantly have concluded they had no choice but to follow him.

Whew! That was close!

"Hey! Are you going to wait for us?" Roxanne called after him.

"Yes, yes, of course." He stopped but looked around nervously.

Le Bret huffed as he caught up to both of them. "All right, out with it."

"What are you talking about?"

"You know very well what I'm talking about. What are you hiding?"

Cyrano scowled, considered the two of them with an arched brow, and finally sighed in resignation. "It's not a what. It's a who."

"Who?" they said in unison.

"Shhh! You *must* keep this quiet. A life could depend on it," he shared in a conspiratorial tone. "Not here."

They followed him to the edge of the small river where they usually swam, and folded their arms.

"C'mon, *ami*, why the dramatics?"

Cyrano paced up and down while the entire story spilled out of him about returning to the woods, the Spanish soldier, his decision to help and trust him, etc.

Le Bret rubbed his chin. "He promised to teach us how to fight?"

"Yes, well, *me*…."

"Oh, no my friend. You mean *Us*!" He clapped a hand on Cyrano's shoulder.

"Ahhhh!"

Roxanne rolled her eyes. "Typical men, always discussing war. Can't you see that violence is what got this poor soul in this predicament in the first place?"

The two boys looked at her with slacked jaws.

"You're not going to tell the adults, are you?" Le Bret begged.

"Of course not, you fool, but I don't like the way you are using him."

"Hey! It's a fair, mutual contract." Cyrano pouted. "So, you just won't help us, is that it?"

Roxanne clicked her tongue. "Don't be an idiot. I could just imagine what his fate would be if the local rabble got him. Of course I'll help. I'm just not going to exploit him the way you two are, especially not to learn the barbaric art of swordplay."

"Oooo, aren't we all haughty," Le Bret cooed.

"Shut up, Le Bret. At least, she is keeping our trust," Cyrano scolded. He then turned to Roxanne. "Then, if you are true to your word, we will need your help filching food and supplies for him."

"Agreed, and we are going to have to come up with a plan complete with alibis for when we are with him."

Chapter 18

The three friends concocted a scheme where they would divide and conquer: every day, Roxanne would visit Marie Feydau and learn sewing from her in order to make clothes for the Spaniard. Her cover story would be that there was a boy–a rather large one–back in Paris that she was fond of and wanted to make him an outfit or two to curry his attention. In the meantime, the boys would start their academic lessons with Gassendi and on the way home, they would make a detour into the woods and bring food to the Spaniard–and linger around for fencing lessons, of course.

Professor Gassendi did not beat around the bush. "Boys, I will not mince words. It is time to treat you like men."

Their ears perked up when they heard this. Were they about to have a frank discussion of adult topics?

"No disrespect to the Curate that taught you before, but the time for superstition is over. You need to learn about scientific fact. A new age of reason is dawning. Scientific reason."

The boys' hopes were quickly dashed.

Gassendi lectured for some time and despite the lack of salacious topics, Cyrano became intrigued. The common sense of the scientific method appealed to his logical mind.

"Science is the true power of the world. Why, without science, where would armies be? There would be no gunpowder, no muskets, no cannons. But it's not just for the benefit of warfare. Medicines, aqueducts, and even today's balloon flights are due to scientific research."

That's true. He started to accept that with imagination and science, practically anything was possible. Even his daydream to travel to the moon could someday become reality. Perhaps the study of science might be valuable, after all.

Just thinking of the word 'imagination' set Cyrano's fertile one into overdrive. He started to wonder what it would be like to travel to the moon. Could he get there by balloon? Would he find air up there? If he made it to the moon, would there be people there? Perhaps not. Maybe it might be inhabited by other creatures. What if these creatures were almost as intelligent as he? They might believe him to be a god. Or a monster.

Just as he started to envision battling off spears thrown by strange little half-human beings, Gassendi's voice snapped him back to reality.

"…and that, my young friends, is how steam can power an engine. Perhaps someday, with the help of Monsieur Branca's invention, we will have steam-powered machines to build us houses or roads."

"Or coaches."

"What was that, Savinien?"

"Coaches, sir. And please call me Cyrano. Steam-powered coaches."

Gassendi smiled broadly. "Exactly, er, Cyrano, exactly!" With that, he closed his books. "Well, that is enough for our first day. Unless you boys would rather sit here and ask me questions instead of enjoying this beautiful weather?"

The boys shook their heads with vehemence.

"I didn't think so. Well, then, *adieu*."

"Au revoir, Professor, and thank you!" They bade farewell as they scrambled out of Gassendi's modest cottage."

Despite all of his daydreaming, Cyrano did not forget about his next tutorial appointment, with the Spanish soldier. Fortunately, the detour from Gassendi's to the woods did not prove a long one.

"And now, *mon ami*, time for our real lessons!" he said to Le Bret once they were out of earshot of any adults.

They picked up the pace and steered their horses to the edge of the tree line at the place where they went in a few nights ago. They dismounted and entered the forest on foot. When the way darkened, they slowed down and Cyrano called out in a stage whisper.

"Spaniard? Are you here? It is I, Cyrano."

A voice replied in the dark of the woods. He could not see the owner.

"Of course I am here. Where else would I be? Dancing with your queen?"

"This Spaniard is a genius at military camouflage," Le Bret whispered.

"Shhh! Quiet, Le Bret!" Cyrano hissed, turned away from his friend and calling out again. "I brought you food. Do you remember our agreement?"

"Yes, I do, but I don't recall including anyone else in our bargain. Who is he?"

"This is Le Bret. He is a friend that can be trusted. Forgive my amendment to our contract, but more students, more food?" Cyrano laid down a generous sack of spoils.

From the shadows emerged a deep sigh. "Very well…."

The soldier emerged from the shadows. He appeared a little less emaciated and Cyrano hoped that was due to his first peace offering. He crouched over the sack and removed a chunk of salted pork and attacked it with relish. After a bit, he looked up at the boys with a sheepish grin.

"Oh, uh, where are my manners?" The Spaniard stood

up proudly. "It seems as though I never told you my name, and if I am to be your teacher, you need to call me something other than 'Spaniard'. My name is Sargento Primero Maximillian Diego de la Mateo, but you may call me Don Diego, eh? Well, then, let the lessons begin, eh? Do you have your *épées*?"

Cyrano and Le Bret indicated their readiness to start with a nod.

"Good, good. You will learn most of your lessons facing off against each other, but for these first lessons, you will face me. You there, did you say your name was Le Bret? Show me the least of your body."

Le Bret, wrinkled his brow and showed him his pinky finger.

"No, no, no, you nincompoop!" Don Diego slapped his brow, "What I mean is turn your body sideways so that your opponent has less to attack. Now, swords at the ready like so, elbow tucked into your side, and the point of the *épée* aimed at your opponent's face. Good, good!"

For the rest of the afternoon, he showed them the basics of fencing: advancing, retreating, thrusting–attacking–parrying–deflecting an attack–and riposting–counter-attacking.

"Now, Cyrano, try *parry tierce*! Good!" Don Diego urged as he reclined against a tree stump while munching on a peach. "All right, that is enough for the first day. The sun is getting low in the sky and the last thing I need is your parents wondering where you are. Tomorrow, I will show you the famous move that made my friend the Duc de Montmorency the most feared swordsman in all of Christendom."

Cyrano and Le Bret looked excitedly at each other at the mention of their outlaw-hero's name.

Chapter 19

For the rest of the summer, a new routine developed–Monday through Thursday, Roxanne would learn music, sewing, and literature from Aunt Marie while the boys learned about logarithms, magnetism, the tides, and how machines worked from Gassendi. That left the evenings and the week's end for typical youthful fun. In between all of this, of course, the boys got almost daily lessons in the martial arts from Don Diego.

Cyrano enjoyed this time the most, not only because of the defensive skills he mastered, but also because of the real-world wisdom Diego imparted between mock-insults.

"Ahhh, *dios*, no! Your lunges are terrible, you dimwit. Let the sword lead you! The *sword*. Remember this, young one, you have no need of a human benefactor. Your best allies are your sword and your own honor. My father taught me that. He was the best swordsmith in all of Madrid. Other people had farms. We had grand forges on our land to create blades that were a work of art. Our craftsmanship was known throughout Europe. That is how I met Henri, your Duc de Montmorency."

As Diego also shared stories of his previous life and the war, Cyrano started to regard him not only as a mentor but also as a role model.

During idle time, Cyrano often thought about Don Diego as well as the other teachers in his life. Aunt Marie,

Gassendi, Don Diego, even Grandfather–they all had one thing in common: they were all alone. Cyrano's well-developed sense of fairness would not allow him to tolerate their loneliness. Furthermore, if he wanted to remain true to the Knight's Code that Grandfather introduced him to, then the welfare of others should not only be his concern; he should do something about it.

They were already working on Don Diego. Roxanne had nearly finished his new set of clothes and she even convinced Aunt Marie to give her a pair of boots that belonged to her late husband. Soon, he might be able to leave the woods, but Cyrano was just not sure whether he should try to convince Diego to make a life for himself in France or to slip back into Spain unnoticed in his brand new set of clothes.

Gassendi's situation would be easy enough to fix. The good professor made it quite clear he was in the market for a wife and it was all too painfully clear who he mooned over. He just needed a little push to get over his reticence. Bashful bachelor, indeed! Cyrano made a mental note to ask Mother to invite *Monsieur* Gassendi to dinner to thank him for his tutoring. He would even serve the food with Le Bret and Roxanne so that Yvette could sit next to the professor. It might be galling to have to wait on her, but if he could just marry off the two of them, he would finally be rid of that meddling imbecile Yvette.

Aunt Marie was not so easy. She seemed fiercely independent as a widow, but she did not deserve to be so lonely, and Cyrano's nature would not tolerate her lack of being taken care of by a good provider. But who? His mind made the leap of logic–his lonely grandfather. *But he is so old!* Cyrano argued with himself. Still, he had known of bigger age disparities between spouses than that. It would not be a December-May romance; more like December-late August.

Furthermore, Grandfather needed someone to take care of him even more than Aunt Marie did. It made perfect sense. They both needed someone; why not each other?

Cyrano was new at playing Cupid, so he would most certainly have to enlist the help of his friends. He would ask Roxanne to inquire on the sly about Aunt Marie's feelings on the matter and he would have to do the same with his grandfather. Alone.

Fortunately, Le Bret was more than understanding when Cyrano asked him to work on Gassendi while he visited Grandfather. Even the artless Le Bret could handle planting the seed in the professor's head that a certain kitchen maid fancied him.

Once he sent the others on their respective missions, Cyrano set out for *Grandfather's* cottage and found him in the kitchen when he arrived.

Perfect opening.

"Hey, Grandpapa, what are you doing?"

"Oh, hello, Young Cyrano. I am preparing some beautiful vegetables from my gardens for a fine little feast. Would you like to join me?"

"Thanks, but no. I had a very big lunch. *Grandpapa*, don't you wish that you had a woman to do that for you?"

Savinien continued his methodical chopping. "Always remember that adulthood means being self-sufficient. Servants are the unnecessary trappings of power; especially in the royal court that your father is so fond of. When you become a true chevalier, you will learn this independence."

"Yes, Grandpapa, I hope so. And no one thinks Yvette more superfluous than I, but what I meant was, don't you miss Grandmama doing these things for you?"

Savinien stopped his cutting and regarded Cyrano for a long time before speaking. "I miss a lot of things about your

Grandmother. When she did things like this for me, it was out of love. I hoped that it brought her joy, the same way that I did things for her out of love. So, in that sense, yes, I do miss that. But most of all, I just miss her."

Cyrano was taken aback by his grandfather's words but he pressed on. "So wouldn't you want… companionship… again?"

Savinien sighed, found a kitchen stool, and smiled at his grandson. "Have you ever watched lightning, Cyrano? When I was in the Gascon Guard, our campaigns demanded that we march through many fields in bad weather. I have seen many storms. I learned to love the sheer majesty of lightning. It could be why I named your horse after the tempest. But in any case, what I noticed during those days was that lightning never strikes in the same place."

Cyrano looked at his grandfather. His eyes were serenely closed. He was lost somewhere in the past.

Finally, Savinien came back to the present. "No one could ever replace your grandmother. It would not be fair to another woman who might expect love in return. I gave my heart away a long time ago."

Touché. Cyrano was tired of losing verbal jousts with adults, but he knew he was not going to win this one. Grandfather's mind was made up.

Savinien must've seen the frown on Cyrano's face. "Look, I realize that I am up there in years, but there is no need for you to worry about me. I can still take care of this farm on my own, and when I can no longer do it, I promise not to be too proud to ask for help. After all…," he smiled, "…that's what grandsons are for."

Cyrano smiled begrudgingly, kissed his grandfather on the head, and said his goodbyes.

"I will be back for a longer visit soon, Grandpapa."

"I know what you are doing, my young one. I hope I know why you are doing it, and I must say…"

Cyrano stopped in his tracks and turned around and faced his grandfather with arched eyebrows.

"…that I have never been more proud of you." Savinien tilted his head serenely. "Never stop doing good, and you will not have to pursue honor. It will find you."

Cyrano flashed him one last satisfied smile. "Thank you. And Grandpapa?"

"Yes, young one?"

"I miss her, too."

Chapter 20

On his way home, Cyrano decided to take a detour and check on Don Diego. He wanted to make sure his tutor had sufficient food and, truth be told, he also wanted to make sure that he did not miss a vital lesson today. His competitive nature would not allow him to fall behind Le Bret in fencing moves.

He dismounted at the edge of the forest as was his habit, and whistled four times—his pre-arranged signal to Don Diego. Something struck him as strange, though. No return whistle came.

"*Don Diego!*" he called out in a stage whisper.

Nothing.

"Don Diego!" he called out in a regular voice.

Still nothing.

He trotted into the dark of the woods, reconnoitered, called out, found what he believed to be his mentor's usual spot, but no Don Diego. Scraps of food and remnants of past meals lay strewn around the floor of the forest and he was sure he was in the right place, but no Don Diego.

Cyrano shrugged—he must be washing up in one of the small streams running nearby, or maybe just taking a walk. Surely, he must get bored staying out here with no books, no music, and only two exasperating boys for company a few hours a week.

He was just about to leave when something on a branch

caught his eye. When he got nearer for a closer look, he saw a piece of white cloth. Suddenly, a chill ran through him. He recognized the cloth as a torn shirt. Worse yet, it had blood stains on it, the blood relatively fresh.

Cyrano was no detective, but his common sense told him to widen his search and explore the ground for more clues. Crouching down and scanning the dirt, he could make out both bare foot prints and several boot prints—circling, crossing over, one trail trampling over another. Obvious signs of a struggle. Waves of panic overtook him.

He stood up and risked the noise. "Don Diego!" he screamed.

Still no answer.

He ran through the forest yelling the Spaniard's name. Hot tears streamed down his face and his deformed nose. Exhausted, and not knowing what else to do, he found his way to his horse and rode back to *Domaine Bergerac*.

Chapter 21

The sun hung low in the sky when Cyrano returned to the *château*. Relief flooded him when he found Roxanne and Le Bret already there—he could count on them for ideas.

"I fear that Don Diego has been taken," he whispered to them in the downstairs hallway, away from prying ears. Roxanne gasped.

"Are you sure?" Le Bret asked with obvious distress in his voice.

"Yes. You know he dared not move out of those woods until we brought him his new clothes; and...I saw signs of a struggle."

"What do we do now?" Roxanne wrung her hands.

"I was hoping you knew."

"If he was taken by the Gascon Guard, they may hang him as a spy. *Mon Dieu!* If he gives up our names, they may hang us as spies, too!" Le Bret clutched at his throat.

Roxanne tsked impatiently, "Don't be ridiculous. The war is over. Spain is even trading with us again."

"True enough, cousin," Cyrano nodded, "but Spaniards are still mistrusted around these parts and I'm not confident in the 'neighborliness' of our typical neighbors."

"Then we need to find out who has taken him," Roxanne concluded.

"If it was the authorities, we might have a chance of freeing him," Le Bret said hopefully.

"If it was an unruly mob, not so much," Cyrano replied in a grim tone.

Just then, a knock came at the front door.

Abel called out from his library. "Yvette, would you please see who is calling?"

"Right away, *Monsieur*...."

Cyrano tried to ignore the noise of the comings and goings and talking at the front door in order to plan the next step with his friends, but he stopped cold when Abel called out to his wife.

"Esp*érance*, I am going into town. Someone needs a lawyer...."

Cyrano led as the three friends trotted after Abel.

"Father, why are you going? It's been years since you practiced private law."

"The constable has captured a man, and he cannot afford a defense attorney. The mayor has asked me to come down to discuss the matter."

"Well, er, what has he done? Is he a desperate criminal?" Cyrano tried to remain nonchalant, but he longed to know if this incident had anything to do with Don Diego.

"Desperate? You could say that, and I do not know if he has done anything other than squat in our forest. That is why they want to speak to me and in turn, I want to speak to him."

The three friends risked a panicked *What do we do now?* glance at each other. Cyrano knew it *had* to be Don Diego. How could they save him? Would they be in trouble themselves?

"Er, *Papa*, are you angry at him for being on our land?"

Abel turned around in surprise. "Certainly not. I'm not doing this just to curry favor from the mayor if that is what you think. He might have summoned me with the belief that I would be a plaintiff. What he doesn't know is that if no one else steps forward, I will represent the man."

That information proved enough to take the edge off of their panic.

"Father, I am glad to hear you say that."

Abel's expression showed equal parts puzzlement and pleasure at Cyrano, but he continued to make his way to the coach waiting for him outside.

The three kept on with their desperate pursuit.

"Er, Father, can we go into town with you? It's been such a long time, and, ah, we want to see…the shops…yes. We promise not to get in your way."

Roxanne added a pair of pleading eyes to tip the scales.

Abel examined each one of them then let out an extra-large sigh of resignation. "Alright. But stay out of trouble. I mean it. Or you will answer not to me, but to Savinien Senior."

"We promise, *Papa*. No trouble." Cyrano looked around at his friends. He hoped his promise did not turn into a lie, but he doubted it.

Chapter 22

Abel entered the legal complex at Perigueux which included the Constable station, Magistrate's courtroom, and a jail be-low. The three teens followed in silence.

He walked up to a man standing behind a small writing desk that Cyrano assumed to be a warrants deputy and intro-duced himself. "I am Abel Cyrano de Bergerac. The consta-ble sent for me?"

The deputy barely looked up from the desk. "He will be with you momentarily. Do you wish to throw these three urchins *en taule*?"

"Hunh? Who's going in the clink?" Abel looked behind him. He then realized that the children had followed him in.

"Ah! I thought you three were going shopping?"

The three teens shrugged sheepishly.

"Go, make yourselves scarce…"

Cyrano searched for a valid protest, but thought better of it and motioned to his friends to follow him out.

"…but don't spend every franc you have with you!" Abel called after them.

Outside, Le Bret and Roxanne looked anxiously at Cyrano.

"Now what do we do?" Le Bret folded his arms.

"I have an idea," Cyrano replied. "If he is being kept right here, then he is in a jail cell in the basement of this building around the back. Hopefully, the cells have at least a little window for ventilation. Hurry, we don't have much time before Father makes his way down there."

Cyrano led them in between buildings and to the dank and smelly alley around the back. Roxanne cringed at the slimy moisture that clung to the bricks. The cobblestones at her feet reeked of urine.

"There!" She found the barred windows they were looking for at the base of the foundation.

"Hurry." Cyrano got on all fours and called into each of the four windows. "Don Diego!"

"Here." The response came from the last window.

Cyrano peered between the bars. "How are you, my friend?"

He could see Diego sitting on a wooden barrel in a dimly lit, graffiti-scrawled cell.

"Actually, I never thought I would find a place more God-awful than my little spot in your woods. I was mistaken."

"What happened?"

"I heard horses at the edge of the forest. I thought it was you three and I got careless. They-a man that looked like a noble and a few of his goons-surrounded me and took me down like a hunted animal. It's my own fault."

"Not to worry. A man is coming downstairs right now to help you. He is a lawyer. If anyone can get you out of here, it's him. He is also my father, so I would appreciate it you would pretend like we never met. He has never beaten me, and I wish to continue that fortunate trend."

"Very well, my young protégé, or should I say 'young stranger'?" Diego mustered a wan smile for his benefit.

Le Bret also knelt down. "Are they feeding you here?"

"If you can call this swill food. I would give my right arm for some of the morsels you used to give me."

"We can fix that. We will be back. Just do or say anything my father tells you, and all will be well. Trust him," Cyrano assured.

"Right, and I never saw you." Diego nodded.

The three teens got up, scurried out of the alley before Abel reached the cell, and headed for the nearest bakery.

Chapter 23

Abel did reach the cell seconds later, and he motioned for the guard to unlock the door.

Diego cautiously exited the cell and Abel moved closer to talk to him.

"What is your name?" he asked, making sure it came out too low for the jailer to hear.

"Diego." He was pretty sure this was not the time or place to give his full title.

Abel spoke quickly as they climbed the stairs to the magistrate's room. "Listen to me carefully, my friend. We do not have much time. I am Abel Cyrano de Bergerac. I understand that you were found on my land. We can discuss the details of that later but right now, you will have to trust me. I have a plan to get you out of here. You will speak as little as possible and when you do, call me Lord Bergerac. Also, I need you to act as if you have known me for some time. Understood?"

Diego looked at him in surprise, smiled thoughtfully, and nodded. "*Oui*, Lord Bergerac."

"Good man."

In the courtroom, Abel recognized the magistrate behind a high bench, the constable to his left.

"Lord Bergerac, so good of you to come in. But this is indeed a curiosity having a plaintiff walking in with a defendant."

"Forgive me, Magistrate, but I had no idea I was a plaintiff," Abel replied with a smile.

"Now I am the one that is confused." The Magistrate rubbed his chin. "Didn't the constable explain the situation when he summoned you? The Game Warden and the Constable found this man on your property. We called you down here to swear out a complaint of criminal trespass and thievery."

"But, Magistrate, why would I swear a complaint against my own farmhand?"

"This man is your servant?" The Magistrate shot an angry look at the Constable who could only shrug.

"I sent Diego out to trap foxes that were killing my chickens. I assumed I was here to pay a fine for him wandering onto De Guiche's lands. We've had some... border disputes... from time-to-time."

The Magistrate could not hide the expression of shock on his face. "Lord Bergerac, I, we, had no idea that this man was in your employ. He had a strange accent."

"An impediment of speech that has afflicted him since his youth. Isn't that right, Diego?"

"Er, *oui*, Lord Bergerac!" Diego nodded with subservience.

The Constable conferred with the Magistrate in hushed tones. Abel saw them hiss arguments back and forth for a minute or so. Finally, the Magistrate turned back to Abel and smiled oily.

"Lord Bergerac, we are pleased that we could clear up this matter. Quite frankly, we thought we might have a foreign spy in our midst. Hehe."

"Well, I am gratified, as well. Come on, Diego, it's time to go home."

They turned to leave when they heard the Magistrate

clear his throat.

"Ahem, many pardons, Lord Bergerac, but… there is a court administration fee…"

"Of course, Magistrate, of course." Abel sighed while he searched his cloak for his drawstring purse.

Chapter 24

Laden with parchment bags of breads and pastries, Cyrano, Le Bret, and Roxanne met Abel and Diego as they descended the steps of the legal complex.

"Young ones, meet Diego," Abel said matter-of-factly as he climbed into his coach.

The three almost dropped their packages in surprise. Cyrano was the first to recover. "Is he free?"

"Yes. Now, get in. I'm sure that Mother has been holding dinner for us for a very long time."

The first ten minutes of the ride home were uncomfortably quiet. Abel, a highly competent lawyer, owed his success in no small part to his ability to read faces. He deciphered the nervous expressions of his son, niece, and their friend with the inscrutability of a sphinx. When he finally broke the deafening silence, the teens visibly jumped.

"Well, I thought the ride home would consist of Diego explaining to me what he was doing in my woods, but somehow, I believe you three might also be able to contribute to the story."

Roxanne's eyes widened as if she'd swallowed three kittens.

Le Bret laughed nervously. "Why, Lord Bergerac, what would make you say that?"

Cyrano's mind raced while his father arched his eyebrow. *The jig is up. He is going to be mad, but he will only get madder if we persist in this charade. Besides, remember Grandpapa's Code; if I want to be real knight, I must maintain my honor with honesty.*

Finally, he sighed. "Yes, *Papa*, you have guessed right. We have been helping Don Diego survive in our woods." Surprisingly, Cyrano felt like a giant had lifted his foot off of his chest.

"Don Diego?"

"Yes, Monsieur...Lord Bergerac...I am Sargento Primero Maximillian Diego de la Mateo. My title in my homeland is...was... Don Diego."

"Did you say 'Sergeant'? Have you been stuck here since the war? *Mon Dieu!*"

"Sadly, yes, but I owe my life to these young ones. You should be proud of them, sir, especially Cyrano. He has the charity of a Christian and the honor of a soldier."

"Indeed!" Abel smiled and arched his eyebrow once more at his son. "Well, I should be very interested in hearing your story, Sergeant. Roxanne! Don't just sit there. Let's have some of those delicious pastries!"

Don Diego left no detail of his circumstances out as they rode home. Abel grunted and tsked at the appropriate points until they were almost home.

As they pulled into the road that led to their *château*, Abel finally spoke. "Well, the problem now, Don Diego, is what to do with you. If I arranged safe passage home for you, there is no guarantee that they would welcome you with open arms. However, I cannot let you subsist like an animal in my forest. I would offer you work around here, but at the moment, I have no room left in my home to offer you." Abel smiled at Le Bret and Roxanne.

"Papa, I believe I might have a solution," Cyrano offered hopefully.

* * * *

The entire family would have to consider dinner that night the most interesting in a long time.

Esperance and Yvette surveyed the foreign Don Diego with suspicion.

Roxanne proudly regarded him as unshaven but dashing in the new outfit that she sewed for him.

Abel, Le Bret, and Cyrano were intrigued by the war stories he recounted. Diego tactfully avoided discussions about Franco-Iberian clashes and dwelled more on his experiences in the Spanish war against England.

Finally, everyone seemed pleased with the plan Cyrano proudly proposed.

"Well…." Abel concluded as he rose from the table. "It is now up to your grandfather to agree with the idea."

Chapter 25

Summer finally drew to a close. Cyrano, Le Bret, and Roxanne had one last evening together before school started again. They talked late into the night.

Grandfather had agreed to Cyrano's plan, and now Don Diego lived with him, taking care of the horses and the grounds (Cyrano hoped he would mind Grandfather as well). Meanwhile, Grandfather had more time to experiment in the kitchen and stay out of trouble with De Guiche. Already, Diego and Grandfather were comfortable enough with each other to trade insults as they worked around the house. Still, the teens found it amazing for two men that once served on opposing armies, albeit not in the same war, to live under the same roof.

Cyrano and Le Bret were excited about going to the *Collège de Bauvais*. Roxanne was not so thrilled. Her bags were already packed for an early morning coach to Paris. She always hated leaving Bergerac, and she especially hated going to a conservative, convent-run school while the boys went to a worldly university. Still, she did not want to ruin their last night together.

They talked about their aspirations.

Le Bret toyed with the idea of studying art. He was especially buoyed by the compliments that everyone had given him lately about his drawing.

Roxanne decided against a filibuster about how pathetic the education system in France proved to be for young women. Instead, she clarified her dreams of being a writer by specifying that she hoped to one day be the first woman newspaper publisher.

Cyrano was coyer about his aspirations. "I dunno what I want to do. As I said before, perhaps I will captain an airship and explore the skies. Or maybe I will be an actor. Or a great scientist."

Le Bret threw a biscuit at him. "Come on! You *know* that you want to be a Musketeer!"

"Shush, Henri!" Roxanne scolded. She then reached out and touched Cyrano's arm, which sent tingles through his body. "Cyrano, you are smart enough to be anything you want to be. I know you long for glory, but try to find the kind of honor that won't get you killed."

Cyrano smiled. "Me? I plan to live forever!"

Another hail of biscuits followed.

Chapter 26

The next morning, the first carriage pulled up to the front of *Domaine Bergerac* shortly after sunrise. Roxanne already waited for it near the front door. As sleepy as he was, Cyrano got up to wait with her.

While the driver loaded her bags in the trundle behind the cab, Roxanne and Cyrano quietly exchanged emotional looks. They had grown closer than they ever were over this summer. No words were needed for them to understand that they hated leaving each other. However, they both knew they had to come up with some kind of verbal expression for their own sense of closure.

"Where is Le Bret?"

Cyrano shrugged. "Still sleeping. I kicked him a few times, but he is not what you would call an early riser. I think he mumbled something about giving you his regards."

"I don't understand why we couldn't just take the same carriage. After all, we are both going to Paris."

The hint of emotion in Roxanne's voice surprised him.

"True, but Le Bret and I don't need to be at the university until late afternoon, and Father thinks the nuns would not take too kindly to you pulling up to their school with two boys in your coach."

"Indeed, especially if I introduced you as *my* partners in crime." They both laughed. "I am glad you and Le Bret included me in your nefarious gang."

"It was an eventful summer," Cyrano agreed.

Roxanne nodded as she looked down at her feet. She then glanced up and stared straight into Cyrano's eyes, which nearly made him wither. "Thank you for including me in the adventure."

Cyrano searched his soul. Was now the time? Should he confess his love for her? What if she rebuffed him? Worse, yet— what if she thought he was joking? He would be devastated. He longed for an opportunity to prove his mettle in battle, but when it came to love, he became an abject coward.

Roxanne must've taken his silence as sadness. "I know, Cyrano. I despise goodbyes, too. Will you write to me?"

"I can guarantee it. Wait! That reminds me. I have something for you." He extended a package wrapped in brown paper.

Roxanne giggled. "I have something for you, as well. It's befitting the stylish Parisian you will be in a few hours." From her bag she produced a tan, wide-brimmed cavalier hat, the same kind that the King's Musketeers wore. "Aunt Marie helped me fashion it. It is made from the finest camel hair."

"Thank you!" Cyrano grinned as he examined the large white plume that went with the hat.

Roxanne gasped when she opened her package. "My favorite author! Thank you, dear!"

Pleased he remembered her fondness for poetry written by women, he was however overjoyed when she reached over, embraced him tight, and kissed him several times on the cheek. That moment would keep him warm throughout the upcoming winter.

"I have to go." She frowned and tried to rush into the carriage before she had to wipe away a tear in front of him.

Cyrano sensed her sadness but he could not get past his

own intoxicated delight from the kiss.

Before the coach pulled away, she stuck her head out of the window.

"See you in Paris?"

Cyrano jumped up, hugged one of the columns that framed the front door of the *château*, and swept his new hat low to the ground in a grand bow. "*Mademoiselle*, once we are situated, I will write you, and we shall make a plan. It will be our next adventure!"

This made Roxanne laugh hysterically. She waved as the coach pulled out of sight.

Chapter 27

Cyrano was in exceptional spirits as he returned to his room to finish his own packing for Paris. Although he bristled under authority, he was always an eager learner. His mind did not focus on academics, though. The cosmopolitan allure of Paris, the promise of adventure, and the hope of romance had his head spinning with delight. He hummed as he packed. Le Bret, asleep on the floor, heard his cheerful noises even over his own dreadful snoring and stirred from dreamland.

"Well, did you tell her?" he asked as he rubbed the sleep out of his eyes.

"Tell her what? What are you talking about?" Cyrano continued to hum.

"I'm talking about Roxanne, you idiot. Did you tell her that you love her? And stop with that frightful droning so early in the morning!"

Cyrano dropped a shirt he was about to stuff in his valise. He was shocked, but he stared out the window casually so as to not tip off Le Bret. "Love?"

"Yes. Do you take me for a simpleton? Love! I know you love her."

"Is it that obvious? Is it as plain as the now-large nose on my face?"

"Of course I know! I am your best friend; I know your every mood."

"Yes, but...." Cyrano shrugged in resigned modesty. "She just loves me as a cousin, I'm sure."

"Need I remind you she is a *distant* cousin, *mon ami*? She is like a third or fourth cousin to you. Barely related by blood! Women are coy things. How do you know she is not just waiting to hear you say the words before she confesses her own feelings?"

"But I am hideous. How can she love one as me, when in her beauty, she could choose any handsome buck that she wishes?"

"Shut up! What are you talking about, your nose? It's hardly noticeable now. Besides, what did your grandfather say? 'Wear your battle scars proudly?' Let me get ready, and once we are in Paris, I will show you that girls, many girls, will find you dashing. So why *not* Roxanne?"

Cyrano did not say another word while he finished packing, but he let his mind wander and his hopes soar. *Paris! Freedom! Pretty girls! Roxanne!*

Chapter 28

The *Collège de Beauvais*—also known to locals as The University—turned out to be a beautiful, white-columned structure built in the Baroque style that was all the rage in 17th Century France. The main building consisted of an open, three-winged layout, with tall, hipped roofs and a cupola at the very center of the edifice. The North Wing housed very high-ceilinged rooms for athletics, such as gymnastics, badminton, and fencing. The South Wing consisted of a four-hundred-seat auditorium, complete with stage. The domed Central Wing consisted of classrooms and offices. Behind this building sat a dormitory for the students and the unmarried professors who chaperoned them.

Bringing your own horses to the college was forbidden, as it would be too easy for underclassmen to slip out of a lecture and enjoy the wantonness of Paris. Therefore, Cyrano and Le Bret had to bid farewell to *Storm* and *Demon* and arrive at the school by Abel's coach.

The boys struggled up the front steps with their bags and reported to the Registrar. There, a harried man with long, curly white hair and black robe took their names and assigned them to a waiting upperclassman. "Dupont! Show these two around. They are in the St. Cyril dorm room."

"*Bonjour, chiots,* my name is Lucien Dupont de Calais. I will be your mentor until I graduate this summer. I will show you around the campus, but first, let's get rid of your saddles. On to the dormitory."

Cyrano and Le Bret had lucked out. They could have been stuck with a sourpuss or even a bully for a mentor, but Lucien proved affable and funny. When he called them "*chiots*", the boys knew it was not meant as an insult, but more of a playful jibe that they were young, naïve puppies.

The gangly blond with the winning smile cracked asinine jokes as he conducted their orientation. Furthermore, as they continued their tour of the college, it became clear that Lucien unceasingly used his personality and charm to ingratiate himself with everyone, be it student body or faculty. It seemed as though he knew every soul on campus, as well as every inside scheme. As they walked, he tossed out tips on who to go to for study help, food bartering, card games, money lending, and contraband items. Cyrano noted his potential as a valuable ally.

Cyrano glanced at Le Bret, his mouth agape. He guessed that he was mar-veling at Lucien's lung capacity. He barely stopped to take a breath chattering through the entire trip until they returned to the door of their dormitory.

The dormitory room was small for two occupants, especially for children of nobility, but it was comfortable enough. Wooden beds and study tables- not of the finest Parisian craftsmanship, but certainly not like a monastery, either. Washing bowl and pitcher. A single tall window to bring in plenty of light to study by, thus saving candles. Fireplace, so they would not freeze in the winter, and low ceiling to keep the heat in. A model of efficiency.

"Don't forget, pups, lunch in a half-hour downstairs in the dining hall. The food's pretty good here. Wash up. No one needs the plague here."

Lucien started to walk away, but caught himself and turned around. "Oh, damn. I was also supposed to tell you all of the rules and regulations around here, but I have to run off. Anyway, I told you the most important things. I'm sure Gargoyle Grangier will cover 'the Commandments' when he delivers his address this afternoon."

The boys stood speechless as Lucien strolled away, humming. Finally, Cyrano swatted at Le Bret's arm. "My friend, we are no longer at the Curate."

"Amen to that."

"C'mon, let's go inside our room until lunch. I want to dash off a quick letter to Roxanne. Isn't it amazing? They have mail delivery every few days here."

"That's Paris for you!" Le Bret smiled.

Chapter 29

After lunch, all the new underclassmen, including Cyrano and Le Bret, were directed to the auditorium where the Dean greeted them.

"Good afternoon, gentlemen. Allow me to introduce myself. I am Jean Grangier. I am not only your Professor of Rhetoric, but I am also the Principal Dean of this institute of learning."

Cyrano and Le Bret looked at each other and Cyrano mouthed *Gargoyle Grangier*, which made Le Bret snicker.

Grangier, who with his stony, unemotional face and ashen complexion, indeed resembled one of the many stone denizens of Notre Dame Cathedral, continued, "In the next two years, if you are not asked to leave, you will learn many things. Rhetoric, of course, but also Science, Business Acumen, Literature, Poetry, Drama, Physical Competition, and Theology."

"Can't get away from the Church, can we?" Cyrano whispered before another pacing teacher shushed him.

Grangier was still on a roll, unaware of the irreverent comment. "Now, let me make myself clear— I know that most of you come from noble and aristocratic families, but I don't really care how close you are to the royal court. If you bring shame upon this school with cheating, lying, stealing, drunkenness, sloth, or lewd behavior in the cabarets of Paris, you will be expelled, and all your papa's money will not change that. Now, you are expected to…."

Grangier droned on about applying one's self to studies, attending vespers, daily mass, and of course, curfew. Cyrano lost attention quickly. He had every intention of proving to his professors that he was talented and brilliant, but he had no interest in blindly adhering to staunch rules. He chafed under the moderate hand of the Curate; no way was he going to knuckle under to the Draconian orders expounded by the iron-fisted Dean here.

Cyrano daydreamed about the cosmopolitan life of Paris he hoped to soon explore—the colorful characters, eccentric poets, and sophisticated restaurants. He fantasized about a beautiful Parisian garden where he could take Roxanne. They would hold hands along the paths, and perhaps more.

The sermon finally reached a conclusion and Le Bret nudged him out of his trance. "C'mon. We are free, for a little bit. We get to shop. There are stores close by. I have our list of books and we have to get loose clothes suitable for the gymnasium. Fortunately, we are not ancient Greeks and exercising *au naturel* is probably frowned upon by The Gargoyle anyway."

Chapter 30

The prospect of exploring stores in Paris helped Cyrano forget about the dean's speech and the oppressive tone it set. He relished the idea of walking the streets of the fashion capital of the world in the stylish new chapeau that Roxanne made for him.

Lucien stopped them before they left the South Wing. "I advise you to travel in a larger group until you are more familiar with the city to ward off pickpockets and muggers. See those three underclassmen over there? Make friends with them and don't let anyone wander off alone."

Lucien's experience again proved spot-on. The three freshmen—Gérard, Pierre, and Edmond—were quite ap-proachable and open to discovering the local streets togeth-er. Cyrano's natural sense of direction came in handy and he became the default leader of the group. They ordered quills, books, charcoal, parchment, ink, and even tights- for exer-cise, from the local merchants to be delivered to their rooms.

One item they would not trust to be delivered was their new *épées* for fencing lessons. The visit to the sword smith turned into the highlight of the shopping excursion as each teen anxiously awaited for their fitting with Monsieur Chat-ellerault, who deftly matched each boy with the custom grip, hilt, guard, and blade balance right for him.

Cyrano thought back to Don Diego. He wondered if he missed his family's sword-making shop. Were they really better swordsmiths than Chatellerault?

Finally, each of the boys strode out of Chatellerault's shop, proudly displaying the blades by their sides, the same way a rooster struts about with his comb and tail feathers.

Wherever smug men swagger, man-size appetites were always sure to follow. Therefore, their last stop before returning to school was a bakery.

Ragueneau's Patisserie, which boasted itself as one of the best in Paris, virtually burst with customers when the boys squeezed into the shop. They walked in and witnessed the jolly owner bantering with customers as he filled paper sacks and parchment cones with cakes, *macarons*, and petit fours. They were patiently waiting their turn when an obese aristocrat and his manservant practically burst into the shop and brushed past them.

"Out of my way. I must conduct my business and get back to the royal palace." He dismissively waved at everyone in front of him. The burly servant pushed people aside so his master need not sully his hands.

"Hey! Wait your turn!" the others protested.

He ignored the objections of the crowd and announced his order. "My good man, give me six almond cakes and six tarts, and be quick about it. The queen is waiting."

The baker nodded quickly, practically cowing, and called for his son. "Raul! Assist me. Please wrap up the Marquis' order and bring it out to him."

Raul, a chubby cherub of a boy, looked only a few years younger than Cyrano. He jumped to attention but seemed clearly intimidated by the brusque Marquis. His hands shook as he filled the order and brought it around from the counter. His eyes were as big as pie plates as he tripped over a flour barrel and spilled the pastries on the floor at the foot of the Marquis.

"Foolish oaf! I am late enough as it is!" the Marquis bellowed and signaled for his servant to grab the boy. "You should be whipped for your stupidity!" He slapped the startled Raul with one of his gloves.

The entire crowd froze in disbelief, with the exception of Cyrano. He grew livid. This brutality was more than he could stand and he could not hold his tongue. "And *you*, sir, should be horse-whipped with your own ruffled collar for abusing your office!"

"How *dare* you, young whelp! Do you know who I am?"

"No, I do not, nor do I care to know, but I know *what* you are—an insufferable bully!" Cyrano helped the boy to his feet but did not take his smoldering eyes off of the aristocrat.

The Marquis sniffed at Cyrano. "Someone needs to teach you your place, boy."

"Who? *You*? Oh, I *beg* you to do so, you bloated bag of bows!" Cyrano unsheathed his *épée*. "This blade is brand new and I am yearning to christen it with the blood of a pompous warthog."

The manservant recoiled at the ringing sound of Cyrano's sword.

For good measure, Le Bret stepped up to his friend's side. "*Monsieur*, you will have to get through me, as well."

This emboldened the crowd and they began to slowly move toward the Marquis, murmuring invectives. "Villain! Brute! Pig!"

Sensing the growing mob threat, the Marquis backed away and finally, with a flourish of his cape, blustered out of the shop sans pastries. The crowd applauded Cyrano.

"That man makes me ashamed to be a nobleman." Cyrano glared at the door.

Suddenly, he felt a slap on his back. The baker.

"Young man, I want to thank you. The Marquis has done this to my customers and my son on more than one occasion."

"I believe he will think twice before troubling you again." Cyrano sniffed with anger.

The younger Ragueneau echoed his father's sentiments. "My name is Raul. I owe you and your friends a debt of gratitude. To that end, let me start with this." He turned to his father. "*Papa*, would it be alright if I treat my friends here to some pies and tarts?"

"But of course! You are always welcome here...ehhh?"

"Cyrano de Bergerac, at your service. This is Henri Le Bret, also Gérard Lafayette, Pierre Martel, and Edmond Le-Clerc." Each teen bowed nobly at his name. "But I insist that we pay!"

"Very well, if you insist. But I insist that you accept the customary discount for friends. You don't mind if I call you my friend, do you, Monsieur Bergerac?" Raul asked.

"Raul Ragueneau, it would be my distinct pleasure."

The boys gleefully chattered and crowed on their way back to the college, cramming pastries into their boastful mouths the entire time.

The dividend of cheap food made Cyrano a hero to his new colleagues, and Gérard, Pierre, and Edmond could not wait to get back to campus to share the legend of how the underclassman from Bergerac stared down a Marquis.

Chapter 31

The next morning, Cyrano and Le Bret woke to a rapping at their dormitory door. By the time their fuzzy brains registered where they were, they heard Lucien's voice on the other side of the door.

"Six o'clock, pups! Be in the dining hall in thirty minutes."

"Six o'clock. *In the morning*? What are we, farmers?" Le Bret moaned to no one in particular.

Cyrano reached for his pocket watch on the night stand. Le Bret had hinted to Abel that he needed one for school. Watches had been around for at least one hundred years but they were still relatively expensive and affordable to only the well-to-do, and alarm mechanisms were still not perfected. So the university ran by the hourly chimes of the tower clock in the Central Wing cupola, supplemented by several cabinet clocks in the halls of the school synchronized with the tower.

The boys began a process that would soon become their morning ritual for the next few months— using a pitcher of water and bowl to wash their faces, throwing on shirts, vests, and trousers that fit into high boots, rushing out the door and scrambling down the main stairs to the dining hall.

Gérard, Pierre, and Edmond joined them at the underclassmen's table.

"Biscuits. Eggs. Eat up. The first class is Mathematics

with Rousseau. He keeps you on your toes," Pierre advised between gulps of milk.

"How did you find that out?" Le Bret wondered aloud.

"My mentor warned me," Pierre shrugged.

As the boys entered *Chambre St. Hubert*, Professor Rousseau barked at them.

"You are one minute late. Now you are interrupting me. Don't let it happen again. Find a seat quickly, open your texts to page four, and try to absorb something besides air."

Le Bret opened his mouth to provide an explanation for their lateness but thought better of it.

By the end of the lesson on prime factorization and exponents, their heads were swimming. Cyrano looked at Le Bret with an expression that said, *We are not in the Curate any more*, mon ami.

Literature with Professor Sorel and Science with Professor Gauthier were more to their liking, and Gassendi had prepared them well for these lessons. Cyrano rattled off facts about the latest findings on the states of matter and invoked an arched eyebrow of satisfaction from Professor Sorel with his ability to convey feeling when reading Latin.

Theology was a required course for every college in Europe by order of the Vatican, with the freshmen scheduled to take it in the *Chambre St.Gregory* before lunch.

"I think that was done on purpose," Le Bret concluded, "So that our rumbling stomachs will prevent us from falling asleep during Professor Mercier's lectures on dogma."

The freshmen, including Gérard, Pierre, Edmond, Le Bret, and Cyrano, all entered the dining hall shaking and staggering at the mind-numbingly tedious lecture they had just endured at the hands of Mercier.

"Le Bret?" Cyrano shook his head slowly.

"Mm?"

"I no longer doubt the existence of Purgatory. I believe we just experienced it firsthand."

"When he droned on and on about the benefits of prayer, I was tempted to pray for Hell to open up and swallow him whole," Le Bret grumbled as he plopped onto a bench at a dining table.

As the freshmen reached for biscuits and soup bowls, several upperclassmen cruised past them and goaded them ominously.

"Look alive, children. Grangier is next for you and he is hungry for freshman blood," needled one senior.

"Hah, yeah, his nickname is The Gargoyle, but I hear he is part Krampus," laughed another as he passed by.

"Heheh, you're hilarious," Cyrano muttered under his breath. He turned to his fellow freshmen. "He's just trying to scare us."

The entire group blinked at him in silence.

"Aw, come on, how bad could he be?"

"My mentor told me he relishes humiliating underclassmen," Gérard offered as he ladled stew into a bowl.

"It makes sense, Cyrano. He teaches Rhetoric. It's like 'The Art of Winning Arguments', and he is the master of it. He won't just undress you with his logic, he'll disembowel you and leave your blanched bones for the vultures," Pierre dramatically declared between bites of bread.

"Well, that's quite an image you paint there, Pierre. With such a command of prose, I'm sure you'll do fine in The Gargoyle's class," Cyrano quipped. "Personally, I'm looking forward to his lecture. As Le Bret here can attest, I love a good challenge." He crossed his arms and legs, "And I've got a rapier tongue of my own."

After finishing lunch, the freshmen filed into *Chambre St. Justine* for the Rhetoric lecture.

"Gentlemen," Jean Grangier began. "Find a seat quickly. The world does not tolerate dawdlers, and neither do I." He paced between the desks of the chamber menacingly. "Welcome to the study of Rhetoric. Here, you will learn the five canons of persuasive speech that were first laid down by philosophers during the ancient Roman empire—invention, arrangement, style, memory, and delivery."

Grangier pointed to a podium at the front of the lecture room. "As a means of putting these canons into practice, from time to time, I will assign you a topic and tell you whether you are to defend or refute a position on that topic, speaking at that rostrum over there."

He smiled wickedly. "And I will take the opposite position, both physically and philosophically over here. May the most eloquent win, but be forewarned: I won't hold back."

The students all looked around at each other in silent fear. There existed nothing more terrifying to a teenage boy than to be embarrassed, especially by an adult, in front of his peers.

Conversely, there was nothing that infuriated Cyrano more than a bully and he sensed a big, intellectual one right now.

Cyrano arched his eyebrow and muttered under his breath, "Real-ly?"

Le Bret had seen that look in his friend's eye before, as recently as Raguenau's bakery.

"Control yourself, *ami*. We just got here," he quietly begged his friend through gritted teeth. "I do not want to get kicked out of here before we have any real fun in Paris!"

If Grangier had noted the exchange, he pretended as if he did not hear them at all. "But we will save that amusement for another day."

The classroom audibly sighed in relief.

"For now, we shall read and discuss the first two chapters of the text. *Without a lot of excess noise*, please...."

Le Bret whooshed the loudest relief as he cracked open his new book on Rhetoric.

Chapter 32

The rest of the scheduled day rolled on and seemed a piece of cake for Cyrano. After Rhetoric class, the boys moved on to the auditorium for Drama, which Cyrano took to like the proverbial fish to water. When Professor Picard, a tall, thin man with angular features, asked for volunteers for a dramatic reading of an Alexandre Hardy play, Cyrano shot up like his seat had springs in it.

Several fellow freshmen could not help but applaud after he recited a passage from "Death of Achilles." Cyrano did not want to spoil the moment or the satisfied smile on Picard's face by admitting it wasn't a cold read and he was familiar with the play through his father's library.

Finally, what better way for underclassmen to end the day than to release pent-up energy in the St. Sebastian gymnasium with Monsieur Durand?

Durand, a swarthy, muscular man with a hardened exomorphic frame addressed the class. "Gentlemen, depending on the time of year, I will give you detailed instruction in a variety of sports suitable for aristocracy such as badminton, tennis, billiards, lawn mallets or croquet as it is also known, gymnastics, and fencing. Yes, it is true that dueling is outlawed, but the practice of fencing in its pure form is not! For this first day of class, there is no formal instruction. You are free to familiarize yourselves with all of the equipment in the gym at your leisure. Our formal lessons begin in earnest tomorrow."

As they milled about the gym with the others, Le Bret whispered to Cyrano. "Don't go for the fencing foils straight away."

"Why not?" Cyrano asked, anxious to show off what Don Diego had taught him.

"Let's not immediately let on how good you are with a sword. The last thing we need is an upperclassman seeing us as a threat. Element of surprise might come in handy later."

"Oooh, there's that crafty side of you again! You are already thinking about tactical advantages. My father should adopt you and he would have that lawyer-son he has always wanted."

"Here. Grab a racquet instead."

Cyrano began to chuckle to himself as he whipped the tennis racquet around.

"What, still laughing at the thought of me being an attorney?"

"No, I was just thinking. If they really wanted us to become good little aristocrats, Durand should be teaching us how to gamble on horse races or cheat at cards!"

Chapter 33

Friday, 30 September 1633
Paris

Dear Grandfather,

I hope that you are well.

Le Bret and I are enjoying our life at the college. We have made numerous friends here and we have settled into a routine. As you might suspect, we each have our preferred areas of study. Le Bret is fond of Art and Math. I don't want to boast, but I sense that I am impressing my teachers in the areas of Science and Drama.

Is Don Diego taking good care of you? Please give him our regards and tell him that we are gradually revealing our mastery of fencing to the rest of the school. More so than any academic accomplishments, our fighting skills have been noticed by our peers and have unexpectedly increased our popularity. I am itching for the opportunity to challenge the older students, but Le Bret still advises discretion.

Speaking of discretion, as you might presume, the dreariest parts of the daily regimen are Theology (I am of course, your grandson, so you will forgive my irreverence) and Rhetoric. Forgive also my candidness, but the Rhetoric professor, Monsieur Grangier, is a belligerent, pompous ass and needs to be reckoned with; but of course, Le Bret is afraid that I will be whipped or even expelled if I best him, so he begs me to be prudent. Besides our time engaged in pursuits that you would feel worthy of a chevalier, our brightest moments are when they expose us to musical studies. I confess that I may never master an instrument like a dutiful nobleman should, but we certainly enjoy singing, particularly when they allow the young ladies from the local music school to accompany us in choir. I will be writing to the rest of the family (and Don Diego) soon, but send them my love. We finally have free time and the adventure of Paris awaits us.

Love,

Cyrano

Le Bret poked his head into their dormitory room. "Oh, Lord, not another letter to Roxanne?"

"No. For your information, this one is for grandfather." Cyrano grew irritated. Le Bret's comment reminded him that he had written to Roxanne three times since they arrived in Paris and she had yet to respond to any of them.

"Good. Now let's get going before they change their minds about letting us out of this prison. The others are waiting downstairs for us."

Cyrano stood up from the small writing table in their room and finished dressing. He buttoned his vest, belted his sword's scabbard, and donned the white-plumed hat that Roxanne made for him. As usual, the hat reminded him of his cousin, and he thought longingly of her again.

As they headed down the main stairs, it occurred to him that Le Bret had not shared his plan for their day. Not that it mattered; any place would be better than the campus.

They joined Gérard, Pierre, Edmond, and a few others outside. As they sauntered off together in search of entertainment, Cyrano put on some brown, gauntleted gloves that were in the military style of the day, not the fashionable white gloves of the upper class. He had great disdain for all the foppish trappings such as ruffle collars, ribbons, sashes, and bows that most of the aristocracy wore, but he was not above looking more ruggedly attractive.

Roxanne offhandedly conveyed to him once that vain dandies repulsed her. He was delighted to hear that her sensible taste proved compatible with his and that made her even more attractive to him. Despite his healthy ego, he vowed never to dress ostentatiously. He always hoped that she took note of it.

The group walked with confidence down the streets of Paris—past the Royal Palace, past Les Halles, glancing in every shop window appreciatively, and acting for all the world like they knew where they were going, which they did not. Cyrano hoped to run into Roxanne out on the street, and despite keeping a vigilant eye open, he saw no sign of her. Therefore, he quickly grew bored with the aimless wandering and posturing. He retreated to the back of the pack where he found Le Bret.

"So, *ami*, what is on today's itinerary? Are we just going to continue to wander around in circles?"

"Well, we need to subtly separate ourselves from the others," Le Bret responded quietly as he slowed down his pace.

"Really? Why is that?"

"You see, at choir practice, I successfully passed that note to Margaux and Emmanuelle without the nuns seeing us...."

"You scoundrel!" Cyrano snickered at his friend's unexpected boldness.

"...So they are going to meet us on Rue Saint-Denis. I don't want the others following us." Le Bret continued undaunted, but with a smile. "Four is 'company' and more are, well, an ugly mob."

Perhaps Le Bret is correct, Cyrano thought. *Paris is a big place with many lovely girls. What's the sense in being lonely and love-sick? Until I can be sure that Roxanne wants to return my affections, I could at least pass the time with a friendly female companion. Hopefully, one that is not insipid or easily impressed by pompous frauds, or pretty boys.*

"Slow down," Le Bret instructed with nonchalance.

The noisy group continued down the boulevard, unaware that Cyrano and Le Bret were drifting far behind. When they were more than a block ahead of them, Le Bret pulled his friend by the arm and led him off to a side street.

They walked two more blocks and turned North onto Rue Saint-Denis. Cyrano looked behind him. None of their group seemed to be following them or even notice they were gone.

After walking a few more blocks, they came upon two smiling girls loitering carelessly outside a perfume shop. These were the same girls that two evenings earlier, Le Bret had nudged Cyrano during choir practice, pointed them out, and identified them as Margaux and Emmanuelle.

Le Bret is a magician. How did he convince these girls to meet us here?

"Hello, *Mademoiselles*!" Le Bret greeted them. "This is my friend that I told you about, Cyrano."

As the girls smiled openly, Cyrano wondered when Le Bret had the time to approach them before today, as he was practically joined at the hip to his friend.

"Emmanuelle, how did you ditch your duenna?" Le Bret asked the brunette.

It was only then that Cyrano noticed that the girls were brazenly walking about the streets of Paris without an older female chaperone to block the advances of the opposite sex.

"I gave her ten francs to go track down chocolate so I can send some to my mother. It will take her all afternoon to find that rare delicacy."

"Ingenious!" Le Bret congratulated her as he offered her his arm. "Then we shall have to be your escorts in her stead."

The blonde named Margaux stood for a moment in front of Cyrano, looking at him. She was very pretty in terms of the fashion of the day, which included a bit more makeup than Cyrano preferred. But she had an upturned nose, round cheeks, and pink lips like shiny flower petals. She was short-er than her companion, but shapely, not petite or frail. Her smoldering dark eyes could command a young man to do practically anything. *Her eyes! Is she looking at my awful nose?* He thought she would turn away in disdain or at least disinterest. That is what his imagination and humility would have expected. To his surprise, though, she smiled slyly and continued to take him in with her appreciative eyes. He felt almost like a draft horse being inspected by an auctioneer.

"Henri tells me you are from Gascon. I didn't know they made men with such big muscles and blue eyes there."

In the face of danger or injustice, Cyrano was unflinchingly heroic, but a compliment from an attractive girl withered him like an old tomato. He feared perspiration showed somewhere on his face or shirt. He searched for one of his typically witty responses—and his long-gone confidence—but before he could even babble a reply, she moved intimately close to his side and softened her voice. "Well, are you my protector for these mean streets today? Parisian girls find great favor in chivalry."

Chivalry! At last something he could understand and latch onto. He couldn't summon the boldness to return her glance for too long, but her proximity ignited the same feel-ings in him as when Roxanne came too close. He found his voice again. "Well, *Mademoiselle*, far be it from me to shrug my duty as a chevalier. My grandfather would never forgive me."

"Then offer me your arm, my brave Gascon guardian, and by all means, squire me around."

Cyrano's natural intelligence and gift for words usually endeared him to his family and adults. He could be witty, comical, charming, and incredibly disarming. He had the ability to talk his way out of a disagreement as quickly as his arrogance and temper could get him into a fight. These talents in no way prepared him for the likes of Margaux. She had an uncanny way of bringing a man's guard down.

Cyrano later mused that she would have made an excellent fencer.

As they walked and laughed, Cyrano's stiff posture disappeared. Was that his 'big Gaston muscles' relaxing?

"Did you have a happy childhood, Cyrano?" Margaux asked as she examined apples outside a farmer's market.

"You could say that. It was certainly comfortable, and my parents are caring folk. It's just that I always craved more."

"Like what?" She brushed her hand against the back of his as he reached for an orange.

"Like adventure." He suddenly realized that in light of the events of last month, his last statement no longer rang true. He tried to change the subject. "How about you?"

"My parents are poor," she said matter-of-factly.

Cyrano narrowed his eyes. "Well, there is nothing wrong with that, but I think you are teasing me. You are certainly not dressed like a pauper."

"My… uncle… rescued me. My parents drink a little too much wine. When I complained about it one day, they became belligerent and threw me out. They claimed I was a bad daughter for questioning them. I had nowhere to go. He found me and took me in, gave me fine things. When he discovered that I had a good voice, he insisted that I study music," she explained as she made faces at herself in a store window.

"Well, he sounds like a saint of a man."

She looked up at Cyrano and smirked as if she just found something quite amusing. "Are *you* a saint?"

Now Cyrano was the amused one. "I have been called many things. Saint was never one of them. I do, however, strive to be a gentleman."

"Being in the company of a true gentleman would be a

new adventure for *me*."

All afternoon, they followed a few paces behind Le Bret and Emmanuelle. They could see the couple in front of them getting very cozy in a very short amount of time.

Taking her cue from them, Margaux stroked Cyrano's arm and asked him many more intimate details of his life. He could not help but prattle on about his favorite subject- himself. He felt so at ease with her that he did not think it odd that she was getting friendly at a break-neck pace.

He suddenly realized that he might not have reciprocated enough. He wanted to show how much he was interested in her. "Where are my manners? I have been talking far too much about myself. What kind of things do you like?"

"Well, I like a great many things." She seemed grateful that the attention turned her way. "Hopefully, we will spend more time together and you will learn that about me." She squeezed his hand. "You could say that I am an Epicurean. Or a Hedonist. What else is life for but seeking pleasures?" She smiled.

The four found themselves at the edge of one of the many public gardens that dotted the city of Paris.

"One of the things I like is *jardins*. Do you like them?" Margaux asked coyly.

"I suppose so…." Cyrano shrugged.

"Well, I like them because people mind their own business there. C'mon." She led him down one of the garden paths.

In seventeenth century France, due to the powerful influence of The Cardinal, staunch public morality was woven into the everyday fabric of life, just as much as immorality ran rampant in private places. Public displays of affection were frowned upon. So much so that a romantic couple could find themselves in the town stocks for a few days just for kissing. The Cardinal conveyed to adults that if they saw such displays openly, they were obligated to admonish or report passion-stricken adolescents, even if they were complete strangers. Therefore, what Margaux was about to do amounted to considerable danger.

She took him under a large, blooming willow tree. The drooping, flowering branches surrounded them like a natural verdant curtain, shielding them from prying eyes.

"Cyrano, I think I have learned enough about you for one day. Enough to know that I like you very much. You are intelligent, gallant, and you make me laugh."

Cyrano smiled sheepishly, but he was no longer afraid to look deeply into her eyes.

"Do you like me?" Her question was almost pleading as she reached in under his vest and caressed his chest. She moved in even closer than she had been all afternoon.

He didn't even finish nodding yes before he found Margaux's lips pressing up on his passionately.

The emotions that Margaux summoned in Cyrano at that moment were very different from his feelings for Roxanne. With Roxanne, he felt love; a love that had a purity to it. He idolized her, but it felt right, natural, and wholesome. He also felt like he was the one in control. If Roxanne never showed signs of reciprocating, he could back off and not reveal his true feelings, and never get hurt.

With Margaux, he was attracted to her on a more primal level. Before he knew what was happening, he had relinquished control to her. She was clearly the pursuer. *Pursuer?* She was coming on so strong with flattery and intimacy, it was more like she was an aggressor, but Cyrano found that, on some level, he liked that. She evoked desire in him, and excitement. After all, they were doing something very taboo in public. That was all part of the allure for him— whether it was at the curate, at home, or at college, he enjoyed breaking rules that he thought were ridiculous.

He felt the little bit of the world under that tree spin dizzily. He wondered if that's how drunks felt, He surely felt intoxicated and hooked, but it was with a different sensation than the pure, innocent desire he knew from this past summer.

He only just caught his breath from her first oral onslaught when she reached up for his face. "I'm going to straighten out that adorable nose of yours...." she said as she pulled his head down to hers and planted her mouth on his again.

Suddenly, he heard a noise from outside the flowing branches of the tree. His heart raced even faster. Did someone catch them?

"Pssst!"

Chapter 34

"Cyrano, are you in there?"

Cyrano relaxed his shoulders when he saw a familiar shadowy figure on the other side of the drooping branches.

"Le Bret? What the…?"

"C'mon, the sun is going down. We have to get the girls back."

Cyrano realized the reason for his friend's urgency. They needed to get back to the college's chapel in time for evening vespers. Attendance would be taken and if they were missing or late, they would lose privileges such as future dates with their new, intriguing companions. He looked down at Margaux.

She huffed and pouted. "Well, I guess we will have to continue this some other time. Promise?"

"Of course. Next Saturday?"

"Thank God. At least I have something to look forward to after a week with tone-deaf nuns. Go on, you two need to get out of here."

"I insist that we escort you and your friend home. It is the chivalrous thing to do."

"You don't have enough time to get us there and still get back to Bauvais. Emmanuelle and I will be fine."

He tried to formulate a protest but she hushed him. "Don't worry, Saint Cyrano. I won't think any less of you." She caressed his face. "Besides, we don't want to raise the suspicions of the duenna." She gave him a much tamer peck on the cheek while Le Bret watched. "Now go. Save your ass."

The boys jumped into a double-time trot and waved goodbye. Le Bret blew kisses back at the girls, who laughed at the boys trying not to trip over their own swords as they ran out of sight.

After five minutes of a dead-on run, Cyrano and Le Bret rounded the side of the East Wing just as the first bell for vespers sounded. Five more rings and the doors to the chapel would shut. They cut across the portico to save time.

"I never got the chance to ask you; how do you feel about today, I mean, about Margaux?" Le Bret puffed as he ran up the last steps of the chapel.

They skidded past a surprised chaplain and dove into a pew as the sixth chime sounded.

"Inspired," Cyrano replied.

Chapter 35

Typically, Sundays at *College Bauvais* were more about boredom than leisure. The Provost's literal interpretation of the Sabbath meant that all work was forbidden, and that extended to formal study. That would be fine with the boys except that mostly everything fun was also prohibited. Only exercise or writing more letters home remained. Instead of holing up in their room, Cyrano and Le Bret found a large oak tree outside the West wing to camp under with paper and quills.

"So who are you writing to? Your parents, Roxanne, or Margaux?" Le Bret asked from the opposite side of the oak trunk.

"Neither."

"You're not doing lessons, are you? If one of the professors catches you…"

"I'm not doing lessons, either. If you must know, I am writing poetry."

"Seriously?"

"I told you last week I was inspired."

"Ahhh, so are you going to recite it to Margaux?"

"Someday, maybe. But for now, this is for me."

Le Bret shook his head and went back to composing a letter to his mother.

The next day, the school routine started anew. During Math, Le Bret noticed that Cyrano seemed unusually distracted. For most of the class, he caught him staring into space. *What is wrong with him? He looks like a love-struck puppy!*

He was concerned that Cyrano would act that way for the entire day, but it was a different story during the next class. Professor Sorel introduced the subject of poetry and Cyrano appeared raptly attentive.

"Poetry can do many things," Professor Sorel began his lecture. "It can motivate bravery, coax lightheartedness, incite anger or despair, and of course, inspire love. Whatever emotion it evokes, most of us have a work of poetry that has deeply affected us in one way or another. Would anyone here like to share with us their favorite poem?"

Cyrano's hand shot up.

"*Monsieur* Cyrano, since you seem so eager, by all means, you may go first."

Cyrano stood up with a scrap of paper, but many times, he didn't even glance at it as he recited.

"Your eyes promise everything
The death of sorrow
The birth of hope
A pledge of intimacy
A vow of life
A covenant of devotion
Will your mouth endorse what your eyes portend?
Indeed, without a word, your lips can proclaim as much,
the greatest desire of my heart
Your kiss a quiet declaration of love"

For a moment, the room remained silent. Sorel seemed slightly stunned and then he cleared his throat. "Er, well done, Cyrano, well done. A very good example of a free-verse love poem. Your delivery was impeccable, but I am not familiar with that piece. Who is the author? Is it a lesser work of Louise Labe?"

"No. I wrote it." He shrugged.

The next thing Le Bret knew, he saw his friend being carted off to the office of The Dean, with Sorel grumbling something about plagiarism.

* * * *

For several minutes, Dean Jean Grangier alternated between eying an indignant Cyrano and looking at the scrap of paper on which he wrote the poem. Finally, he addressed him.

"Your face is familiar to me. You are in my Rhetoric class, no?"

"Yes, sir." Instead of feeling terror, Cyrano's gut bubbled with fire. He knew he had done nothing wrong. He struggled to keep his responses respectful.

"Professor Sorel has given me the details of today's class. He told me how impressed he was with your incredible ability to compose poetry." He narrowed his eyes. "Forgive me if I am not moved similarly, but I have a cynical nature. I believe that you lied about the incident. It would go better for you if you are honest with me now."

"I am always honest," Cyrano said matter-of-factly. "But it would help if you told me what you are talking about. Why do you think that I am incapable of writing a simple rhyme?"

Grangier leaned forward across his desk. "That 'simple rhyme' as you call it, possessed an incredible sense of feeling, intuition, and imagination, not to mention the rest of the classic qualities of romantic poetry. No upperclassman could ever hope to possess the talent to create such an exceptional piece, let alone a mere freshman. You *must* be lying. Did you do so to impress your peers, or perhaps to play a prank on your teacher?"

"Chevaliers do not lie. Perhaps I am not your typical underclassman, Dean, because the work is mine. I thank you for the flattery."

Grangier's brow furrowed and his face flushed crimson. "Oh, so now you fancy yourself some sort of knight? Well, knights are not disrespectful, either, boy."

"I fail to see how I am being disrespectful, sir. I am merely defending my honor, which appears to be under attack here."

Grangier narrowed his eyes.

Cyrano decided not to stop even at the risk of angering him more. In fact, his quick intellect engaged into an even higher gear, searching for an ironclad defense. He was not about to embarrass himself with the sappy excuse that he wrote the poem yesterday in a lovelorn reverie. Surely, a gargoyle like Grangier would ridicule him like he did many others in his Rhetoric debates. Still, there had to be a way to prove his innocence. Suddenly, he had it.

"If I may sir, I can put it in terms that I know you are familiar with— the concepts found in your very own Rhetoric class. In Latin, I believe it is pronounced *habeas corpus;* if I am guilty of stealing the work of another, present the proof. If my poem is as good as you say it is— and again, I thank you for the compliment—then surely, it was published already. Therefore, it should be found in a book of poetry somewhere in a library as comprehensive as the one here at the University. If you can produce its twin in a volume here, then I am guilty as charged. I will gladly wait in the dining hall while you search for the evidence. I am famished."

Cyrano knew it did not help his situation by being so smug, but he felt emboldened by the knowledge of his own innocence.

"Get out of my office."

Ever impertinent, Cyrano bowed deeply as he backed his way out the door.

* * * *

Grangier was doubly enraged, firstly because this young whelp refused to be intimidated, and secondly, because he recognized the boy' attempt to hoist him with his own petard of Rhetoric.

He knew it would take years to prove that Cyrano was guilty. He was also well aware of Abel Bergerac's reputation as an exceptional lawyer. He had discovered that Cyrano was his son when he reviewed his registration documents. He certainly did not want to tangle with the wrath of Lord Bergerac if he tried to expel Cyrano.

I will have to avenge your insolence some other way, Young Cyrano, Grangier thought.

For the time being, I will have to console myself with disgracing you in my Rhetoric class.

As he pondered, his mind turned over a devious idea.

"Moreau!" He called out to his assistant in the ante-room. A second later, a skittish little man popped into the room, ready for another order.

"Get me the upperclassman named Antoine De Guiche."

Chapter 36

Cyrano strolled into the dining hall and plopped down next to Le Bret.

"Where the hell have you been? I've been worried sick." Le Bret demanded.

"Oh, The Gargoyle just wanted to tell me how much he admired my writing talents." Cyrano smiled and then perused the lunch fare on the table.

Le Bret sighed. "Well, I knew I couldn't keep you out of trouble forever. Tribulation seems to follow you like a shadow. You didn't get expelled, did you?"

"You cannot expel an innocent man, *mon ami*." He tapped the side of his nose and winked. "However, to dispel any remaining shadow of doubt surrounding my good name, I will simply have to replicate the feat again and again."

"Huh?"

"I'm going to write more poems. Lots of them. Apparently, I have a knack for it."

"Hahahahh! Well, perhaps you will need more inspiration. You may be a gifted poet, but I am an even better fortune teller." Le Bret closed his eyes and touched both his temples. "And I foresee a trip to the cabarets of Paris in our future!"

"Let's get through the rest of the week first, my friend."

* * * *

A knock came at Grangier's office door.

"You sent for me, Dean?" Antoine De Guiche poked his head into the office warily.

"Come in and close the door."

"I want to start by saying that I had nothing to do with the hazing of that freshman—"

"Shut up and sit down. I want to talk to you about something else. A job of sorts; ideal for a young man of your… talents."

"A job?"

Grangier unveiled a cunning smile. "Yes, and it could benefit some of your relatives, as well."

"Relatives?"

"Good lord, De Guiche, are you some sort of parrot? Stop repeating everything! I am talking about your cousins, Ruffe and Odo. Can you send for them?"

"What, the ones you said were too poor and stupid to come to the college?"

"I believe what I said was 'underprivileged', but perhaps a 'scholarship' could be arranged for them if they were willing to help you with this task."

"I will get right on it. Wait…" Young De Guiche paused from rising and narrowed his eyes. "What do we have to do?"

"Have you heard of an underclassman named Cyrano?"

"Who hasn't? He has made quite a name for himself. The other freshmen look up to him. A friend to all. A genius in science, not to mention his prowess in drama class."

Grangier winced. *There is no one harder to take down than a braggart that can back up his own boasts, especially a popular one, but I have to put that Gascon boy De Bergerac in his place.*

"That may be, De Guiche, er, *Antoine*, but he is still a detriment to this fine institution of learning and I need you

and your cousins to help me teach him a lesson in humility...."

Chapter 37

No one ever suspects when they step into a viper's nest, and the same was true of Cyrano.

A week passed since the day he was accused of cheating by Grangier and it seemed to him there would be no further repercussions.

His focus on science and writing more poetry, he thought about Roxanne, who still had not written back to him. She represented the inspiration for his poems, not Margaux. Although Margaux sparked a passion in him, he would rather have that passion with Roxanne, someone with whom he had such a history. Yet, whatever poetry he wrote, he did not think it good enough for her ever to see it; if ever he mustered the courage to tell her his true feelings.

Cyrano sat in Rhetoric class thinking about words that rhymed with rose when he suddenly realized that his classmates were laughing.

What's so funny? Wait, are they laughing...at me?

"Well, *Monsieur* De Bergerac, are you waiting for a special invitation?" Grangier taunted him.

"Hmm?" Cyrano looked around for someone to clue him in.

"You're up. He wants to joust with you, at the debate podium," Le Bret hissed at him.

"Debate? Me?"

Cyrano was still a little disoriented as he walked up to

the front of the room. By the time he reached the podium, he had snapped to attention. Fully aware of his situation now, panic gripped him, as he felt unprepared. Sensing a chance to conquer yet another bully in Grangier, he shook off the fear quickly.

Remember, you wanted this!

Week after week, Cyrano would watch as yet another of his classmates would go down in flames at the hands of Grangier's withering logical onslaughts. He would lure them in by allowing an opening argument and then completely dismantle their position until they found themselves entrapped in self-contradiction and feeling like utter fools as they skulked back to their seats. He hated the fact that The Gargoyle gloated at how he humiliated his students and called it an education.

Don't be an idiot like that.

Cyrano felt not unlike his hero, the Duc de Montmorency, getting ready for a fencing duel.

It is a challenge of honor, after all....

"The subject, De Bergerac, is Moral Imperatives. I shall defend, and you shall refute this statement—It is never right to lie."

Several students moaned or whistled softly as they recognized the subject matter to be chock full of moral landmines. If Cyrano wasn't careful, at best, he could be defending dishonesty; at worst, he could look like a religious heretic.

Oh, no, you don't. I'm not falling for that. "By all means, Professor Grangier, you may go first."

Grangier smiled cunningly. *That was your first tactical mistake, Bergerac.* "Truth. It is pure. It is what God wants from us and it is always moral. To tell the truth is to seek the Divine. The opposite of truth is Deceit, and the path to damnation. When God discovered that Adam and Eve had eaten from the forbidden tree of knowledge, he confronted them. If they had not lied to God, they would not have been banished from Paradise." *Talk your way out of that, boy.*

Cyrano paused for dramatic effect and then began. "I do not dispute what you have said."

Grangier widened his eyes in surprise and then narrowed them smugly. *Victory.* "Well then, there you have it—"

"I said…that I do not dispute what you say, at least not the intent—innocent and simplistic although it may be—"

"Simplistic!" Grangier thundered.

"However, I do ask for proof of what you say."

"Proof!" Grangier seemed clearly rattled.

"Yes. Proof. How can you prove that the truth is always the correct choice?"

"Hahaha. Why, the proof is manifold. There are literally thousands of examples of it in The Bible."

"Ah, The Bible. But is it not true that man wrote The Bible, and is it not true that men habitually lie?"

"Man may have recorded the words in The Bible, but it is divinely inspired by God." Grangier pointed heavenward.

"Ah, but who told us that? The men who wrote it? Perhaps they were lying just so that more people would buy their book. I know many authors who would admit that they aren't above doing that if it meant more royalties for them."

Grangier waved his hands impatiently. "Even if one cannot provide irrefutable physical proof that God does not want us to lie, it does not change the fact that lies hurt others and can cause spiritual damage."

"Ah, but Professor, you did not ask me to dispute that the truth is the higher moral ground; you specifically asked me to refute the statement that it is *never* right to lie. Now if your grandmamma—I am sure she is a dear woman—if she wore a hideous brooch to a dinner with the Cardinal, and she asked you how it looked. Would you tell her it looked appalling? I think not."

"Ah, but I would. Honesty would set me free."

"Really? Even if the truth would do more harm than a lie? What if she was a sensitive woman, whose pride could be easily wounded? What if the brooch was a family heirloom and to dislike it amounted to insulting your family heritage? What if she asked you right in front of the Cardinal and she might be greatly embarrassed if you did not call the brooch exquisite? What harm is there in telling a small lie to her in that situation?"

"You would have me tell a lie in front of a Cardinal? That is preposterous. Only the truth would do!" Grangier was nearly yelling.

"Then let us examine our terms. What is truth? Do we have a definition?"

"Truth is defined by what is fact."

"Oh, like the facts in a case of law?"

"Yes, indeed."

"You mean when one witness in a case says that they see a man steal a loaf of bread, and another witness says something completely different? How can we decide on a case if there is disagreement?"

"By simply calling more witnesses until a majority agree on a fact."

"So then, truth is not universal; it just depends on a majority. For example, if you were surrounded by a field of atheists that insisted there was no God, then that statement would be true because they were in the majority?"

"No, that's not what I meant."

"Good, because I would hate to think that if the majority of students in this class believed that you were a pompous ass, and only you and I thought the opposite, that we would be wrong."

Grangier was fuming but refused to open his mouth in fear that he would dig an even deeper hole for himself.

"No, Professor. I do not dispute what you say about the value of truth. I do, however, believe that there is a deeper meaning to truth than just universal agreement on facts. Truth is sincerity in your actions, even if it means that you have to tell a little white lie to make your loved ones feel better. Truth is a fidelity to your ideals, whether an army of atheists or one single Cardinal tells you that you are wrong. Truth is an honorable choice of free will rather than a moral imperative—"

"That is quite enough of your insolence! Sit down, Bergerac!"

Cyrano tried to contain the smile as he picked his way to the back of the room. Fortunately for the rest of the students, the period ended soon after and with it, their feelings of discomfort. Cyrano was not through with Grangier, though.

At dinner, he ate in his room; not to be anti-social, but because he was busy and did not want to be disturbed. He was busy writing. Not another letter, not another poem, but a play—with a certain dean as the main character.

During Drama class the next day, Professor Picard asked if any student could provide an example of a contemporary play that would demonstrate the literary vehicle of satire.

"I do, Professor!" Cyrano announced with eagerness. "It is a play called 'The Pedant Duped'. I happen to have the script in my possession."

"Really, Cyrano. Hmm, I cannot say that I am familiar with that work. Who is the author?"

"Um, it's a very colloquial work, but popular in Gascon. May I?"

Picard nodded, and Cyrano recruited several friends in

the class—Le Bret, Gérard, and Edmund—to come to the stage to play characters in a reading of the first act of his script.

Gérard bowed deeply and began reading as the narrator. "The Pedant Duped is the story of a fat, bald, repulsive professor who lusts after a much younger lady. Do not despair, my friends, as he gets his just desserts."

Cyrano took on the role of the professor's rebellious son who is his rival for the affections of the young Genevote. He constantly outwits his father and wins her hand.

As several boys in the audience snickered and whispered, "Grangier. The play is about Grangier," Picard stopped the read-through.

"Er, yes, well, thank you, Cyrano, but we are running out of time. That was…interesting…."

Cyrano bowed and returned to his seat in the auditorium amid chuckles and hoots from his peers. He crossed his arms in triumph. Suddenly, he heard a voice behind him.

"Monsieur Bergerac, please accompany me to my office." The Provost of the College stood in the doorway and had seen the whole spectacle.

Luckily for Cyrano, the walk from the auditorium to the Provost's office was a short one, because the silence felt awkward and the suspense gnawed at him.

"Close the door," the Provost called behind him as he slumped behind his desk.

Cyrano stood before the desk. He felt relieved that it wasn't Grangier that heard his play, but he was still in deep trouble. The Provost outranked even Dean Grangier and now, he was about to toss him out. Cyrano thought ahead to how his father would take the news of his expulsion. His eyes blinked to prevent any angry tears that might be conspiring to form.

"Sit down. This isn't the Inquisition." The Provost sighed wearily. "What do you like to be called?"

Cyrano hesitated in surprise. "I'm sorry, sir? It's just that no adult has ever asked me that before. Cyrano. I like to be referred to as Cyrano."

"Well, Cyrano, perhaps it is because no adult ever bothered to treat you like another adult before today."

Cyrano was surprised to see a smile on the Provost's face. Not what he expected but he was still wary. He sat down.

The Provost continued. "I can assure you that if you are at this institution, then you are indeed an adult and with that goes all of the privileges...." The Provost saw Cyrano give a large visible exhale. "....and all of the responsibilities, too. Cyrano, I have heard quite a bit about you from many sources—other students, instructors, even your father when he enrolled you here. They all think highly of you. Perhaps right now, Professor Grangier would disagree with all of them, but I thought it important to form my own opinions. So, over the past two months, I have been observing you, as I do many students here. Here is the thing that sets you apart in my mind—I see a lot of me as a younger man in you."

"Are you going to tell me that you were an arrogant, cynic, dissident that finally stopped jousting with windmills and learned to conform?" Cyrano crossed his arms.

"Ah, I see that you have read Don Quixote. Excellent book!" The Provost smiled, and then shook his head, "No, what I was going to say was that I see in you a young man of high character that finds it hard to compromise his ideals, and because I was like you, I do not expect you to do so. But that is where our similarities end. You have so many more gifts that I envy—a sharp intellect and big heart to go with it. Throw in the mix the fact that you have the soul of a warrior, and you have a formidable recipe; one that, if the dough were to rise correctly, would yield a fine leader of men."

The Provost got up from his chair and looked out the window into the grassy quad of the college below. "Now, you may dispute the authority of The Bible with Professor Grangier—yes, I heard about that incident as well—but one thing you cannot deny and that is the book contains much wisdom, including this quote: 'To those whom much is given, much will be required.' Do you understand what that is? You have a responsibility to reach your full potential. I am not going to stand here and debate with you whether The Gargoyle—yes, I know his nickname—is a bully or a villain, but I cannot help you reach that potential if you make it too easy for him to force me to expel you. Am I making myself clear?"

"Yes, sir." Cyrano's anger had dissipated and for once, he actually cared about staying in school. *Grandpapa*, Father, and now the Provost. The list of people Cyrano wanted to make proud of him was growing.

"So we have an agreement. You will refrain from antagonizing Professor Grangier, and I will help you choose your path, be it scientist, militiaman, or poet."

"Musketeer, sir. I wanted to be a musketeer, but you have me thinking: why can't I be all three?"

"Indeed. Why not? I believe you can be anything you set your impressive mind to, but only if you exercise discipline over your impulsive nature. You may go now."

Cyrano scrambled to his feet and was ready to practically skip out of the office until the Provost called after him.

"And Cyrano, just in case you also want to try your hand at interpreting the law like your father, that bit about being treated like an adult does not mean that the rules do not apply to you. You are still expected to make curfew, and avoid fights, drunkenness, and women of easy virtue."

"Yes, sir!"

Chapter 38

Cyrano limped through the rest of his classes for the day. After that, the weekend officially started for him and Le Bret.

They ambled down to the main floor and checked the wooden sorting box for the space reserved especially for their mail. There were several envelopes from home, even a package of treats, but still no letter from Roxanne.

Le Bret must've seen the disappointment on Cyrano's face. "Ach, I can't stand that long puppy face of yours anymore! Either we are going to a cabaret this weekend or we are going to find Emmanuelle and Margaux. Or both!"

Le Bret excused himself to make connections and clandestine plans. Cyrano went back up to their dorm room to nap until Le Bret returned with a clear plan of action. No doubt he would need his rest to keep up with whatever shenanigans his friend had in store for them. Cyrano was clearly exhausted from the mental gymnastics of the past few days, between sparring with Grangier and the soul-searching the Provost put him through. He had all but shrugged off the Gargoyle's distastefulness, but the hopeful message from the Provost still rang fresh in his mind.

As Cyrano skimmed through letters from Mama, Grandfather, and even Don Diego, several freshmen passed by his doorway. Each one stopped to give him a word of encouragement. He half expected Gérard, Pierre, and Edmond, but this was more, many more than just them.

"Cyrano, good job yesterday in Rhetoric. You really showed up Grangier."

"Hey old man, the way you made fun of the Gargoyle today in Drama, that was outstanding!"

One from a teen named André was especially heartfelt. "Cyrano, I want to thank you. I used to dread going to Grangier's class every day. But you proved to me that he is just human. He can't humiliate me if I don't let him."

After more than a dozen such acknowledgements from his classmates, he closed the door for some private reflection—and a few minutes of shut-eye. Perhaps the Provost was on to something. Maybe he *was* a leader. If so, he needed to make sure he was leading in the right direction and not straight into a ditch.

He had just dozed off and was in the middle of a dream where he was the fearless, swashbuckling Captain of the Musketeer Guard when Le Bret burst into the room and stirred him from his fantasy world.

"Wake up, my friend. We are in for a treat! D'Artagnan has offered to show us the nightlife of Paris!"

Chapter 39

A carriage waited outside of *College Bauvais* for Le Bret and Cyrano and whisked them away from their safe street down the wide avenue for many blocks; Cyrano estimated perhaps fifteen, until it reached the Opera House. Once they passed around the opera, they then traveled through several shady neighborhoods until the driver finally stopped at a street called *Rue de Clichy*. When the boys got out, they attempted to pay the driver but he refused.

"*Count* D'Artagnan has already paid in advance. I would not dishonor him by taking one *franc* more."

The boys stood on the street for a moment, searching for a familiar face. All they saw were some very used-looking, obnoxiously painted women who leered at them with knowing looks. Suddenly, they heard some raucous singing coming down the street towards them. Finally, they saw a group of musketeers singing the bawdy songs, with D'Artagnan in the lead.

"Oyyy, cousin! There you are!" D'Artagnan hailed them with a boisterous voice. "Fellows, these are my young protégés that I was telling you about. Le Bret and Cyrano."

The rest of the musketeers greeted them in a cacophony of noise, back-patting, hand-shaking, and even drunken hugs.

D'Artagnan then bid adieu to his brothers in arms. "Farewell, musketeers, I won't bore you with this babysitting duty. It is mine alone to bear." He put his hand across his heart in mock drama. "I will see you back at the garrison. Do not wait up for me!"

"Ha! Do not wait up for *us*!" Athos said. "I doubt very much that these two will keep pace with you for very long, and you will be home well before us."

D'Artagnan put his arms around both boys' shoulders, probably as much for his own balance as for chumminess, and slurred. "Pay no attention to those hooligans. Tonight is the beginning of a very important education for you. Come, let's be off!"

D'Artagnan continued to usher them down the street in that same three-abreast fashion. "Now, where would you like to start? La Porte? Zerbé's? Oh wait, I know just the place. *Le Corsaire*!"

They trudged on until they were in front of a wide, Baroque-style building with a large wooden sign hanging over the door. The wood had the figure of a pirate carved into it. An improbable amount of laughter, music, and general noise seemed to be barely contained behind the front door. A surly-looking character guarded the entrance, but softened as soon as he recognized D'Artagnan. He nodded at him knowingly and opened the door for them.

The inside of *Le Corsaire* was dark, raucous, smoky, and overrun with the smell of cheap Parisian perfume. Somehow over the loud music, D'Artagnan made his whispering understood to a waiter. Seconds later, the waiter pushed a sleeping drunk off a table and cleared it for them.

Le Bret, Cyrano, and D'Artagnan sat facing the stage so they could watch the musicians—a guitarist, lute player, flutist, and a singer—perform rollicking numbers. A waitress wearing a typical wench's fluffy blouse and tight corset slinked up to D'Artagnan. It was clear to Cyrano by the very familiar way she greeted him that they were well-acquaint-ed. "Well, if it isn't the *Count*! Give us a hug, dear, and tell us what you and your cadets here will have."

"Oh, we're not cad— Ow!" Cyrano received an elbow in his ribs from his friend.

"Perhaps we can get our first taste of Parisian wine," Le Bret whispered to him.

D'Artagnan tented an eyebrow at them. "I know what you two are up to. Tonight is an 'education', not a complete debauchery. Therefore, you will be having something milder, perhaps mead, and I will be the only one partaking of wine tonight, thank you. And there are quite a few pipes floating around in here, too. No American tobacco, either. That's not for young lungs."

The boys slumped their shoulders and pouted but when the drinks came, Cyrano was satisfied that they were engag-ing in 'adult activity' in an 'adult environment'. The beer-like mead proved so weak, it only produced a warm sensa-tion throughout his body, but not even so much as a buzz.

It was clear that D'Artagnan knew all of the tricks and he would take good care of them tonight.

After a few rounds of drinks, all three were inspired to do some impromptu singing and banging on the table in time to the music. This was all encouraged by the musicians, es-pecially when they were tipped. It seemed typical of what all the other patrons in the cabaret were doing.

If they did not know the song that was being played, they would pass the time in animated discussions of fencing techniques, women, and politics. D'Artagnan would speak to the boys in a stage whisper when the subject came around to the royal court.

"I'm telling you one thing. As young noblemen, you need to be careful who you trust. When your grandfathers pass, saints preserve, you will both have titles such as I do. So, you've got to be mindful of all of the shifting alliances swirling around you, or you might find yourself with a less-than-desirable commission in the army- or worse, find your lands seized by the crown. Believe me when I tell you that there is much intrigue in the Queen's court. And the Cardinal is more than what he appears to be."

The boys looked at each other. Cyrano was held spellbound by the cryptic nature of D'Artagnan's tone.

"So here is where your education starts. Not by doing manly things; there's plenty of time for that—"

For the fourth time at least that night, D'Artagnan was interrupted by a different comely waitress who came by to stroke his back or touch him in some manner. He would barely pay them mind and would continue talking. "...the cabaret here is a microcosm of the royal court, perhaps even the whole adult world. If you can develop savviness here, you can apply that same shrewdness and vigilance in your lives in general."

D'Artagnan pointed his chin towards a wobbly patron. "Take a look at that poor soul over there."

"Who, that old drunk?"

"Yes, he is so drunk and careless, he is totally unaware that he is about to become a victim. Watch what happens."

The drunk leaned over a pretty waitress who had called him over to a bench she sat at with a few other strident customers. As he bent over, completely enthralled with the tickling she was giving his face, he didn't even realize that a pickpocket behind him was relieving him of his purse-bag of coins.

D'Artagnan quickly pushed himself up from their table. "Excuse me for a moment, fellows."

Le Bret and Cyrano watched with slacked jaws as

D'Artagnan deftly picked his way around sailors, sots, and strumpets to grab the thief by the scruff of the neck with one hand. With the other hand, he retrieved the stolen purse. After a few harsh words were exchanged, D'Artagnan wagged his finger in the thief's face and sent him off with a boot to his britches. He then called out to the drunk. "You dropped this, *ami!*" Then he tossed the purse back to him.

The drunk smiled, waved, and slurred his appreciation. "I muss be more careful, *monnssieur*. Obliged!"

Now back at their table, D'Artagnan finished his lecture. "Lesson Number One: never go to a cabaret alone. Lesson Number Two: always pay for your drinks in advance so no underhanded proprietors can surprise you with a hefty bill after your sobriety has abandoned you. Once your pre-payment is exhausted, it's time to go home. Lesson Number Three: unlike our friend over there, always know where your wallet is."

Two girls not much older than them wandered past the table and flirted with the boys by caressing their arms and nuzzling their ears.

D'Artagnan cleared his throat. "Ahem, Lesson Number Four: if a strange girl seems too good to be true, she probably is; refer back to Lesson Number Three."

The girls moved on to the next set of customers.

"Finally, Lesson Number Five: never start a fight if you are clearly wrong or clearly outnumbered. Unless you have some musketeers to back you up." He smiled mischievously.

Suddenly, a very pretty girl plopped herself in D'Artagnan's lap and kissed him for an uncomfortably long time. When he finally came up for air, he finished with one last bit of advice. "Oh, and I forgot to mention. Lesson Number Four only applies to strange girls. If they are more… familiar… well then, trust your instincts!"

He turned back towards the girl with a twinkle in his eye. "Excuse me for one moment, Collette. I must send my protégés back to their monastery."

Collette eyed them with surprise. "Are they really monks? What are they doing here in this den of iniquity?"

"Hahaha, I'm kidding, my pet! They are college boys, not monks. But they have taken a vow of chastity and sobriety."

The boys started to protest, but D'Artagnan held up a hand. "Now, now, we can continue this some other night! But for tonight, don't break your curfew, and get some rest. I understand Le Bret has already planned more fun for you tomorrow."

Finally back in the same carriage that they came in, Cyrano interrogated Le Bret on the way back to their dorm. "Okay, what was D'Artagnan talking about? What other plans do you have for us tomorrow?"

"You'll see. All in good time."

Chapter 40

Saturday broke with sunshine and promise. Fall slowly yielded to winter, the days mostly colder, but Mother Nature did not give in to Old Man Winter without a fight, and brought out a spectacularly unseasonable Indian Summer day.

"Wake up." Le Bret stood over his friend and nudged him. "You are going to want to use the bath."

"Hunh? Why?"

"Because you will want to look, and frankly, smell appealing to our company today."

When Cyrano returned from freshening up, he found Le Bret putting on cologne and his finest clothes.

"How much money are you bringing today?" Le Bret asked as he struggled with his boot.

"Well, it would help if I knew where we were going…."

"I'll tell you in a moment. Bring about ten *francs*. Better yet, a few *pistoles*."

The boys devoured a quick breakfast and headed outside. To Cyrano's surprise, D'Artagnan waited for them, standing in front of a wooden-bed, horse-drawn cart similar to the ones farmers used in Bergerac. Strangely, this one smelled like gunpowder.

"Good morning, cousin!" D'Artagnan greeted with a sunny air. "Here you are! Do you have my finder's fee?"

Le Bret nudged Cyrano. "Yes, indeed. We have two *pis-*

toles for you."

"Ahhh, many thanks." D'Artagnan bowed mockingly. "The gaming tables were not friendly to me last night after your exit."

Cyrano was still bewildered. "We're taking this cart? Where did you get it from?"

"Oh, I just 'borrowed' it from the garrison. One of the perks of being one of the Queen's musketeers. Now take good care of it, and Elsie, too. They need to be back by roll call at sundown."

"Many thanks to you, cousin! Where are you off to in this part of town?"

"You know the convent around the corner from your college?"

"St. Mary's? Yes."

"Well, I am off to perform a valuable service for the Church."

Cyrano was always bemused by D'Artagnan. "Oh, and what might that service be?"

"Well, I thought I would interview some of the novices and make sure that they are really committed about their vows."

"You rascal!" Le Bret guffawed.

"Seriously, I have some legal business to do for Grandfather, so don't worry. I am not at risk of being excommunicated. Yet. Have fun, you two!"

Once D'Artagnan strolled away, Cyrano resumed his cross-examination. "Le Bret, I love your devious mind, but where in heaven's name are we going?"

"Swimming. Did you put extra clothes in that bag as I instructed you?"

"Right here."

"Good. Now we are off to *Ragueneau's Patisserie* to

buy some lunch, and then to pick up our companions. I shall drive, as Elsie seems to have a peculiar connection to my family."

Laden with sacks of baked goods that young Ragueneau insisted on giving them at a steep discount, the boys took the cart a few blocks further where Emmanuelle and Margaux awaited them.

Le Bret smiled down from the driver's bench. "I see that you have successfully eluded your duenna again."

"'Tis a pity, Henri. Someone told her the wrong date and she inadvertently ate meat on Friday, so she is doing penance all morning." Emmanuelle laughed.

The boys clambered off of the cart and helped the girls on, Emmanuelle on the front bench with Le Bret, and Margaux in the back with Cyrano. He blushed when her hands lingered on him when he hoisted her up into the cart by her waist. He was suddenly struck with panic. *What if Roxanne was on this street right now and saw us? Would she be angry? Jealous? If she cared at all, it would serve her right for not writing back to me.*

Cyrano looked around the street. No Roxanne. He hopped into the back with Margaux.

Le Bret pointed the cart northwest and they headed for the less-populated outskirts of Paris where the River Oise ran.

Chapter 41

While Le Bret drove, Cyrano and Margaux quietly talked in the back. As far as physical closeness went, she took up right where they left off at their first encounter.

"I'm sorry if I seemed a little forward when we first met, Cyrano, but I took an instant liking to you. I do want to know more about you. What is your family like?"

Cyrano talked fondly of his parents and his grandfather and what a great place Bergerac was to grow up in.

"Your father and grandfather worked for the royal family. Are they very rich?"

Cyrano shrugged. "My family has more titles than we have gold, but we are reasonably well off."

With that information, Margaux seemed to draw even closer to him.

Cyrano suddenly remembered D'Artagnan's advice on Lesson Number Four. He needed to know more about this girl before he rushed in any more like the proverbial fool.

"Tell me more about your family, your life. You told me that your uncle rescued you?"

"Well, it is very distressing for me to talk about," Margaux's voice trailed off, but she smiled at him, "But I know that I can confide in you."

"Of course!" Cyrano insisted gallantly.

"You see, my mother and my father were terrible drunkards. When Mama died of influenza, Papa beat me when he was angry, and he was angry all of the time after Mama passed." Margaux sighed. "My uncle took pity upon me. Well, he is not my blood uncle. He was a friend of my mother's. Anyway, he took me in, fed me well, and bought me fine clothes and perfume. If it were not for him, I might be in a dirty old orphanage instead of a fine Parisian apartment."

"He sounds like a noble fellow," he offered.

Margaux looked off into the distance with no expression on her face.

They left the urban sprawl behind and finally arrived at an open, unfenced area that didn't seem to belong to any of the adjacent farms. A line of trees sat at the edge of this field, and then beyond the tree sparkled the clear, blue Oise River.

They pulled up to the banks of the river and set up a picnic blanket under a tree and ate lunch. They laughed and made plans to enjoy other things in Paris, such as theater, orchestra, fairs, and parades.

Finally, Le Bret announced it was a good time to go swimming.

"Fine, then Margaux and I are going behind those trees to change. Now, no peeking!" Emmanuelle warned as she stood up.

Margaux smiled and whispered to Cyrano. "No, we wouldn't want you to see our… qualities."

Cyrano bit his lip. He was not sure how to respond. He was accustomed to Roxanne's innocent teasing, not to this type of outright flirtation. He wasn't sure what kind of rejoinder might result in a face slap.

When the girls emerged from the tree line, the boys could see that their bathing outfits stopped above their knees and exposed their shoulders. Not much skin was actually uncovered but the boys were mesmerized, nonetheless.

For almost two hours, they frolicked in the water, the

boys showed off for the girls by diving and holding their breath under water. The girls taunted the boys for their exaggerated bravado. Finally, they broke off into couples.

Margaux took Cyrano by the hand and led him off to her preferred privacy spot, under a tree. As soon as they were out of sight of the others, Margaux wasted no time. Cyrano contemplated sharing some verses of his love poetry with her, but she made it clear that flowery speech was not necessary and perhaps a waste of time. She practically ambushed his face with her lips.

Cyrano was charmed by her advances, but he felt as if he could hardly catch his breath. "My love, I am flattered by your eagerness, but I feel like I am drowning in your kisses. Can we come up for air for a minute?"

Margaux smiled playfully. "I like that you called me your love. Are you falling in love with me, Cyrano?"

"I have to admit that I am a novice when it comes to experiencing these emotions. I can tell you one thing, though—no other girl has made me feel exactly like this, and if this is what love is supposed to feel like, then… I love the feeling."

"Well, I cannot deny it anymore, Cyrano. I am in love with you."

Hearing those words triggered a raging argument in Cyrano's mind.

Isn't this what you have always longed to hear from a girl?

But we practically just met!

Maybe Le Bret is right; even with this nasty big nose, women find me irresistible. Oh, what is this power I suddenly have over women? I must use it prudently, else they will be throwing themselves at me everywhere….

He looked at Margaux. It seemed to him that she was swept up in the moment, as well. *Is she panting with passion?*

He could also see that her neck and chest were flushed. She started to pull down on the edges of her swimming blouse, baring far too much skin to him.

"Oh, my, it is so warm for a November day," she said between breaths.

Cyrano reached over and reluctantly stopped her from exposing herself more. He shook his head, but said nothing else.

Margaux's eyes narrowed and her face tightened, but it quickly changed back to smooth. "Yes, you are right to be sensible, Love." She made a show of covering up her modesty again. "It's just that I feel like I want to trust you with *everything*, including myself. Because if we... love... each other, I *can* trust you, right?"

"Of course."

"Then I have something to confess. I wasn't quite honest with you before, but I want to come clean. My... uncle... he is not as gallant as you think."

Cyrano's nostrils flared. "He doesn't beat you, does he?"

"No! No, nothing like that, but he is constantly reminding me that I would be an orphan on the unforgiving streets of Paris if it weren't for his kindness. So, I feel like I am constantly obliged to him... and his friends. I cannot say no to him when he asks me to entertain his 'associates', as he calls them."

Cyrano narrowed his eyes. "What does he pressure you to do?"

"Well, sometimes, it is just something as simple as dancing and singing for them. That is why I am in music school, to perfect that craft. That is also where I met Emmanuelle. Sometimes, these men want the dancing to be... provocative." Margaux's eyes fixed on the ground. "Sometimes, they want even more."

"That scoundrel! I want to thrash him. Now!" Cyrano smacked his palm with a clenched fist.

"No, no, you mustn't," Margaux grabbed both of his shoulders, "He is far too powerful a man. He is very, very close to the Cardinal. He could crush you, and any hopes you have of a career."

"I am not concerned about my future. I am concerned about your well-being."

"Even if that future could be with me?" Margaux looked up at him expectantly.

Cyrano's gallant heart pounded. Things were moving so fast. In one afternoon, he had discovered that a girl had fallen for him; she was also a damsel in distress, and now, he was talking about a possible future life with her. It was the stuff of childhood fairytales and he was immersed in it.

Margaux held him tightly and spoke between kisses. "No… my love, we must be cautious… and cunning. With your help… I can escape his clutches for good, and we can be together. Would you like that?"

"How can I refuse you?"

"Then you will help me?"

"You can count on me."

"Good, my love. I have a plan, but we must keep it our little secret. We cannot even tell the others. Agreed?"

Cyrano hesitated. He'd tried keeping Don Diego a secret from Le Bret and had hated it. But this was different. Margaux's life was clearly in danger and Le Bret was a bit of a blabbermouth. If he shared it with the wrong people, there was no telling who it would get back to.

"Agreed."

"Oh, Cyrano, you have made me the happiest girl!" Margaux hopped in place. "Soon, I will be free, and I will never have to leave your arms. Now let's get back to the others."

The four of them changed back into their traveling clothes and Le Bret drove them to the center of Paris to discreetly drop off the girls.

Before they parted company, Margaux whispered into Cyrano's ear. "Now, I have your address at school. When I am sure of the timing, I will write to you and give you the details of my plan." She gave Cyrano one last kiss to seal their covenant.

"Very well. Please be careful."

Margaux looked both ways down the Rue as if she wanted to make sure she was not being observed or followed. Then, she and Emmanuelle strode off into the crowd.

"Well, what was *that* all about, Romeo?"

"A gentleman never kisses and tells. Hey, I never knew you read Shakespeare."

"The English fellow? Professor Sorel says that one day, he will be required reading for our children."

Just then, a familiar-looking female figure passed the periphery of Cyrano's vision. Definitely familiar, but not Margaux.

Was that Roxanne?

He turned his full attention towards the young woman's direction. She was still too far away for him to confirm it was her. One thing he could clearly make out, though, was that she was accompanied by a young man with wavy hair about their age as well as an older woman.

Cyrano pounded on his friend's shoulder. "Le Bret! Drive the cart. That way. Up the street!"

"What?"

"Just *do* it!"

Le Bret obliged without another word.

"Stop," Cyrano finally commanded, and he jumped

down to survey the street.

"Are you mad? What the hell are you looking for?" Le Bret looked around as well, but he did not see anything that would cause such a fuss.

I lost her in the crowd. Cyrano sighed. "Nothing. I thought I saw something."

"Well, we've got to go. I've got to get this cart back to D'Artagnan, or we will all be cooked!"

Cyrano nodded slowly and climbed onto the front bench with his friend.

If it was Roxanne, what was she doing with that boy? The same thing I was doing with Margaux? At least her duenna was with her, so her reputation is safe. But is this boy the reason why she has not written back to me? How could she forget me so soon? Cyrano rubbed his own arms as he hugged himself. *How could I have forgotten about* her *so soon?*

Chapter 42

By the time they got back to their dorm, they were exhausted. They narrowly made curfew and the scare sapped their energy. Cyrano was doubly tired because of his inner turmoil. They stayed up for a short time talking and then collapsed into a deep sleep.

When he woke Sunday morning, Cyrano's mind was still a storm of conflicting emotions, torn between missing Roxanne and feeling discarded by her, intrigued by Margaux but unsure that she was a soul mate. Not to mention feeling true concern for her safety.

With all this upheaval, he had lost the drive to write romantic poetry. He concluded that he needed a physical outlet for his stress instead of a creative one. He headed for the gymnasium.

When he arrived, there were several first- and second-year students in fencing garb. Cyrano ignored them and headed to the far end of the room. He stretched, picked up a foil, and practiced his positions and techniques.

Cyrano hoped to go unnoticed, but some of the boys hooted to get his attention.

"Oy, Cyrano, come here," called the one Cyrano knew as Bernard, "We are about to start a little competition. Would you like to join us?"

He shrugged. This was the price of shenanigans; you become popular with your peers. He really needed to blow off steam. "Why not?" He finally answered as he walked towards them.

"Round robin tournament," Bernard explained, "The four duelists with the most victories will meet in a pair of semifinals and then a final. We are using right of way rules. Okay?"

"Fine by me," he agreed with nonchalance.

Ten boys, perhaps the ten best fencers in the whole school, faced off against each other. Two matches occurred at the same time, so that the other boys waiting for their turn could act as judges.

Cyrano made short work of two eager but inexperienced freshmen, Rainier and Auguste. Bernard was tougher for him because of his strength, but Cyrano easily found a flaw in his game. Instead of fighting brute force with brute force, he used ceding, give-way parries to his attacks, which left Bernard's body wide open to counter-attacks after the parries.

Next was his friend, Pierre, who was not a bad swordsman. However, he lacked a killer instinct and was easily psyched out by Cyrano's superior footwork.

Marcel came after Pierre, but he was way too slow to stop Cyrano's whip-like counter-riposte move.

And so it continued throughout the tournament. Cyrano proved to be either too strong, too quick, or too clever for his opponents. Often, he toyed with them until he found a weakness and then he exploited it.

After the first round, his record was nine-zero. Roberte, an upper classman's, was eight-one. Maurice and Jean-Louis were both at seven-two.

In the semifinals, Cyrano drew Jean-Louis and Roberte faced off against Maurice.

Instead of wandering off after they had been eliminated, every one of the boys stuck around in the gym to watch

Cyrano and marvel at his skill.

The rules were that the first fencer to reach three touches became the victor of the match.

Jean-Louis was a crafty competitor, altering his strategy from their bout in the round-robin. In that first round, Jean-Louis just tried to plow straight ahead at Cyrano, an approach that worked against many of the others because they tried to parry his attacks with the foible–the weak, flexible end of their foils–instead of with the *forté*, the stronger portion at the base of the sword, which led to quick, easy points leads for Jean-Louis.

Thanks to Don Diego's coaching, Cyrano was too smart to fall for that tactic and he easily dodged the attacks with strong parries called 'beats', and then won the point on counter-attacks.

In their second meeting, though, both Jean-Louis and Cyrano proved cagier. They waltzed back-and-forth on the *piste*, the in-bounds line where a bout is fought. The other boys hooted and whistled as the two of them traded attacks, parries, ripostes, and disengages. Cyrano was leading two touches to one, but Jean-Louis was a tenacious defender and prevented him from landing the last winning touch.

Finally, Cyrano saw the weakness he was searching for. Jean-Louis was a good swordsman but his thinking was two-dimensional. His foil was always at the same height, and so were his attacks. Cyrano devised a plan.

He raised himself up on his toes for his next advance. Jean-Louis adjusted the end of his foil to point towards Cyrano's chest. Cyrano attacked and then feigned to leave his upper chest vulnerable to a counter-attack. Jean-Louis saw this and lunged. At the last moment, Cyrano crouched low and the attack went overhead. *Passé!*

With the miss, Jean-Louis' chest was left wide open and

Cyrano finished the match with a 'flick' attack, a quick whip of his foil across Jean-Louis' torso, instead of a touch.

"Amazing! Well done, Cyrano!" The cheers came from the spectators.

"Nice whip," Jean-Louis smiled graciously between pants.

"I was lucky." Cyrano returned the courtesy.

Surprisingly, Roberte disposed of Maurice quickly in the other semifinal match, and he observed Cyrano intently as he fought Jean-Louis. Looking for weaknesses, just as Cyrano did.

The finals bout was then set between Roberte and Cyrano. Roberte turned into an even more formidable opponent. He had been lucky enough to attend the French Fencing Academy, and even traveled to Italy to train under students of the great Italian fencers of the last century, Agrippa and Grassi.

The rest of the boys surrounded the *piste*, in anticipation of a memorable event.

Cyrano and Roberte saluted each other in the traditional fashion with their weapons, foil to nose and sweeping down.

From the very first move, the crowd yelped and rooted.

The final round was the most complex and technically flawless of the bouts and both Roberte and Cyrano performed like magicians.

Coup followed by parry, followed by riposte, followed by counter-parries and counter-ripostes. The footwork was a smooth ballet of check-steps, cross-overs, and lunges.

Soon, Cyrano and Roberte were tied with two touches apiece. Cyrano could see that the elder boy was tiring, but he needed a gambit to win an advantage. He remembered that everyone agreed that the rules would include 'right of way' priority. That meant that if two fencers accomplished a touch, or touché, simultaneously, then the fencer who was the aggressor would get the point. The advantage always went to the attacker, so he decided to exploit this.

Cyrano mounted a blistering, ever-advancing forward attack that never retreated. Sure enough, it led to a double touch, and per the rules of right-of-way, Cyrano was awarded the point, two-one.

Roberte requested a time out to compose himself. Both boys were sweating profusely, so Cyrano welcomed the chance for some water. During the time-out, Roberte's friend whispered something in his ear. Le Bret happened to be passing the gym and he heard all of the raucous cheering. When he stuck his head in, he saw his friend in the middle of the crowd and he immediately concluded that Cyrano must be in the midst of the match.

So much for laying low and keeping our fencing skills secret....

The bout resumed with another salute and the tactical chess match also continued. Roberte clearly benefited from the break as well as the coaching from his friend. Cyrano had planned on winning the match with the same plan he used against Jean-Louis–stay low and hit low. This time, however, Roberte was ready for it. He matched Cyrano's posture and took the fight low. Using the right-of-way rule to his own advantage, Roberte scored a very low touch with an incredibly low knee-bend attack. Two-two.

Le Bret marched over to the crowd and called a time-out for Cyrano.

He was surprised and delighted to see his friend. "Hey, I thought you were napping."

"I have a sixth sense for foolishness. Besides, how could you dare have a match without your best friend as your second?"

"I thought your ugly mug could use a beauty rest."

"Very funny. And what happened to remaining inconspicuous? You realize that getting involved in this stunt means that every upperclassman who thinks he is a great swordsman will be looking for you. You might as well have had Aunt Marie embroider 'challenge me to a duel' on your vest."

"Change in plans." Cyrano shrugged, "Even the greatest generals adjust on the fly."

"Well, since our cover is blown, we might as well shove all of our chips into the pot. You have a plan to win this last point?"

"Are you thinking what I am thinking? That day in the woods with Don Diego and that tree trunk got in our way?"

"Indeed! Do it, and do it quickly, before all of your energy is gone."

The bout started again, and Roberte wasted no time going on the offensive and keeping his attacks low.

Cyrano was ready, and batted it away, but there was no opportunity for a counter. Losing their breath, both boys recovered by backing up to the very opposite ends of the *piste*. It was clear to each of them that the match was going to end on this very next clash. They both built up a head of steam and charged at each other.

Roberte went low and Cyrano was ready. At the last moment before impact, instead of going low, he leaped high into the air in a movement called a *flèche*, and smacked Roberte on the top of his head with his foil. The crowd of boys jumped up in amazement. "*Touché*! Bravo! Cyrano, well done!"

They joyously swarmed around him in a cacophonous celebration.

Roberte was clearly angry, but more at himself than

anyone else. He recovered well, and shook Cyrano's hand.

"You showed great skill," he conceded.

"I salute an equally great competitor." Cyrano bowed gallantly.

"If I see you on the streets of Paris, I think that I owe you a drink."

"Or two!" Cyrano joked. "I look forward to a rematch."

"You can count on it, my friend." Roberte slapped him on the back and the rest of the crowd did the same.

Chapter 43

Cyrano enjoyed his ever-growing celebrity for a good two weeks or so. Everyone was talking about the bold first-year student who bested Grangier in a battle of wits, trounced all comers in fencing, and could top it off by being the next royal poet laureate.

One November Friday, Cyrano and Le Bret were bounding up the main staircase to get to Professor Gauthier's class when they ran square into two blocks of concrete named Ruffe and Odo at the top of the landing. Cyrano would have recognized that bowl haircut and those nasty teeth anywhere. Tucked safely behind them was Antoine De Guiche.

"You freshman need to be more careful. You wouldn't want to go tumbling down the steps and crack your idiot skulls open, would you?" De Guiche sneered.

Ruffe grunted a smile and shoved Cyrano, as Odo did the same to Le Bret. Cyrano was too shocked at the sight of his familiar attackers to mount a swift defense. He and Le Bret fell back and down a half-dozen steps before they recovered.

"I wish I was the one that broke that nose of yours," Ruffe called down to them.

"Be seeing you around school." Antoine smiled. All three of the thugs laughed.

Cyrano got up to rush at the boys, but before he could mount one step, they were gone.

"Just as well." Le Bret narrowed his eyes. "They had the tactical advantage. Remember what D'Artagnan said. I told you we would become marked men if you showed your fencing prowess."

"No, those three knew us from before. Remember the wolf hunt?"

"Ohhhh, yeah! The one in the back. The Count De Guiche's spoiled little spawn, right?"

"Right. And the other two tried to mug me right in front of my house."

"Oh, the ones you told me you threw apples at? What in the world are those two dolts doing in a place of higher learning?"

Cyrano shrugged. "Don't know, but things just got more...complicated. We will have to watch our backs."

Chapter 44

Despite having a bull's eye on their backs, the boys muddled through for a few more weeks unscathed. Thanks to Le Bret, there was not another major confrontation with Antoine and his bodyguards. Cyrano was never one to back down from a fight, but if Le Bret even saw a glimpse of the Gang of Three, he would distract or redirect Cyrano before he knew they were coming.

In almost a month, Cyrano had seen Margaux only once. The night of that encounter, the air hung full of intrigue.

At her suggestion, they met for dinner in a quiet restaurant in a section of Paris halfway between the college and her apartment. Margaux was dressed and made up in a very sophisticated manner. When Cyrano commented on her appearance, she replied that she needed to look mature so that people would mistake them for a much older couple. Even so, she looked around furtively and asked Cyrano if he could tip the waiter so they could eat in a private, curtained salon. Cyrano felt like he was on a date with a spy.

It was not a night for silliness or lighthearted conversation. Margaux exuded a combination of heat and desperation. The entire night, she sat close to him, gripped his arm constantly, and spoke in whispers.

"I brought you here tonight because I have some news. The time for my deliverance is almost at hand, and as I predicted, I will need your help to bring my plan to fruition," she breathed anxiously in his ear.

Cyrano was delighted to hear he might have a hand in winning her freedom. "Anything, if it means you are out of that man's clutches."

Margaux smiled wryly. "I am relieved. He has been particularly demanding and…cruel…lately. Fortunately, after several years of trying, I have finally been able to track down a cousin who is willing to take me in…until you finish school…and we can be together permanently."

"That's good." Cyrano tried not to shudder when he thought about an enduring relationship with Margaux. Was he thrilled or frightened by the idea? He still wasn't sure. Now was not the time to discuss or dispute it, though. "What can I do to help?"

"How much money do you have?"

"Huh?"

"I will need to hire a cab to get to her house." Margaux smiled. "She lives on the other side of Paris, far away from my 'uncle' and his friends."

"Oh, of course. I will need some to pay for our meal, but I will gladly give you the rest."

Margaux wrapped her arms around him and covered his face in kisses. "Thank you, my savior!"

They parted ways with the promise of a more permanent reunion soon.

That was weeks ago. Cyrano had not heard anything from her. Until today. Between classes, he went down to the office that housed the mail cubicles and found an envelope addressed to him in a delicate handwriting. The stationery was of fine quality and smelled like Margaux's perfume. He didn't wait for privacy to read it.

My Dearest,

Our plan is about to unfold. Soon, I will hire a coach to take me to my cousin, and I will be free of that monster who calls himself my uncle. I must impose upon you one more time, though. My cousin's landlord is very strict. He wants to charge her more for another border.

Can you please help us?

Please send fifty francs to the address below and I will have a place to stay with her until I can send for you.

I love you!

22 Rue de Jouy

Cyrano folded the letter and thought for a moment, Fifty francs. That will nearly drain his reserves, unless he wrote home for more money. That could take almost a week by the time the letter got there and back. What if Father said, "no"? That would be more wasted time. Maybe if he talked to him face-to-face and was honest with him, that the money was not for him?

He couldn't go home until the weekend, and that was almost as long as a letter would take.

I could try to track down Father, here in Paris, but how would I even know if it was one of the days that he worked at the palace? Would he be angry that I disturbed him? Would the musketeers at the gates even let me in?

The musketeers! D'Artagnan!

Cyrano ran off to find Le Bret.

"So, we are going to sneak out of school, in the middle of the day, risk expulsion, run down to the garrison, find my cousin, convince him to help us find your father, and then convince *him* to go to the bank and give you fifty francs? For a girl?" Le Bret looked at him incredulously.

"A girl in distress," Cyrano added.

"Are we just going to stroll out the front door in broad

daylight like we are book salesmen, or do you have some sort of plan?"

From behind them, the Registrar burst out of his office into the hallway where they were standing. He had an armful of packages.

"Dupont. Dupont! Where is that lazy jester? I need him for an errand! Dupont!"

"I think one just came our way. Play along," Cyrano whispered to Le Bret as he turned around.

"Uh, I believe that he is ill, sir. Is there anything we can do to help?"

The Registrar scrutinized him. "You are the one from Bergerac. Cyrano, right?"

"Yes, sir."

"Hmm, I have heard of you. Good things, I might add. Smart. Leader. Well, I don't usually allow first-years to be messengers, but I am desperate. You'll do."

Le Bret nudged Cyrano in the ribs.

"Uh, sir, this is Le Bret. Do you mind if I take him along? For protection?"

The Registrar eyed Le Bret suspiciously and then shrugged. "I guess that's not a bad idea. Two would be safer. Very well. I need you to deliver these manuscripts and letters to these addresses. It may take you a few hours, and knowing voracious boys, you will probably stop for lunch, too. Remember, this is a privilege, so don't abuse it."

"Yes, sir!" they responded as they ran towards the main doors.

"And you will be expected to make up the work you missed!" he called after them.

Chapter 45

The packages slowed the boys down, but they managed to huff their way to the musketeer garrison.

D'Artagnan listened to their story and injected some sensible reasoning. "Whoa! I understand your urgency, but I'm not so sure this is such a well thought-out plan. I'll tell you what we should do. I will borrow a horse and cart again. First, we will deliver your packages quickly and then instead of barging into the palace, let's take a trip out to this *Rue de Jouy*. I want to make sure your lovely lady has made it to her cousin's. If she has, I will lend you the fifty francs for the rent and you can pay it in person. No need to get your father involved in this, Cyrano, at least, not yet. And mind you, I said I will *lend* you the fifty francs. I expect to be paid back, eventually. Who knows? Perhaps a musketeer could talk some sense into that greedy landlord and I could save you some money."

* * * *

D'Artagnan urged the military cart down the streets of Paris at an alarming rate. He had hitched two horses for more speed, their trip further enabled by the fact that the side of the cart was stamped, "munitions." Other drivers and pedestrians alike gave them a wide berth, assuming the vehicle was loaded down with gunpowder.

Jumping out of the cart here and there throughout the center of Paris, Cyrano and Le Bret made quick work of the college deliveries–a publishing house, a lawyer's office, and another college.

Relieved of that burden, the three headed southeast in search of the address in Margaux's letter.

Finally, they came upon *Rue de Jouy*. The street was not at all what Cyrano expected–seedy, populated with several stray animals, and refuse filled the gutters. Cyrano, Le Bret, and D'Artagnan looked at each other in shock and started searching for building numbers. Several grubby taverns sat on the street, complete with sleeping drunks propped up against them on the sidewalks. In between the saloons were dilapidated buildings, each one in greater disrepair than the last.

Scanning the houses, Cyrano's gaze fell upon #22. He had quietly hoped it would be some sort of quaint, clean oasis in the middle of this block of despair. It was not. The tiny, two-story house was just as ramshackle as the rest of the area.

D'Artagnan gave Cyrano a look of concern. "You all right?"

Cyrano nodded.

"Do you want us to go with you?" Le Bret asked apprehensively.

He shook his head. "No, this is my task."

He hopped off the cart, headed for the front door of #22, took a deep breath, and knocked.

A few seconds later, he heard footsteps approach, and the door opened. He was relieved to see Margaux's face.

"Hey!" He smiled at her.

She did not return the smile. Instead, her face registered shock and then anger.

"*Merde!*" she muttered under her breath. She glanced quickly into the hallway behind her and positioned her body to block the view inside. "What are you *doing* here?" she chastised him.

"I...I don't understand. Isn't this your cousin's apartment?"

"No, it's not." Tears started streaming down Margaux's face.

Far behind her, Cyrano caught a faint glimpse of a man inside the house. "*Mon Dieu!* Is this your *uncle's* apartment?" he demanded.

"No!" Margaux closed the door behind her before the man could see what was going on and she pushed Cyrano down the front step. "No, it's not. You weren't supposed to come here."

"What is going on here? If that man is not your uncle, then who is he?"

"It doesn't matter who he is." Margaux sobbed. "I'm sorry! I'm sorry! I deceived you, and that was wrong. I was desperate for money. The truth is, I was supposed to be long gone before you ever showed up here."

Cyrano reeled as if he had just received a punch that reached the very pit of his stomach. "So, what is it, then? What was your game? Is that man in there your flesh-peddler that you are trying to escape, or is he just a customer?"

She slapped his face. All of the charm and warmth she had showered on him was gone. "I am not a tramp!"

"Ow! Really? Well, you certainly weren't acting like a lady around me. How could you do this? I was almost convinced that I loved you and now I find out you aren't who you say you are, and I even get a slap in my face for my troubles? Oh, I get it now! You are simply a confidence artist! How foolish could I be to think that with this nose of mine you could find me attractive? So, am I the only idiot that fell for this scheme, or do you and your lover in there fleece naive marks like me on a regular basis?"

"He is *not* my lover!" Margaux admonished. "He is my husband."

Cyrano was dumbfounded. All of his angry, snappy retorts left him. He just looked at her. Still hurt, but bewildered now, as well. "I could easily have you arrested for a stunt like this. You see my friend in the cart? He is a musketeer."

Margaux folded her arms in front of her and lowered her eyes contritely. "Look, I am sorry that I broke your heart. I won't lie and say that I didn't mean to hurt you, but it was nothing personal. You were just a casualty of my need." She looked up to meet his eyes with a pleading look. "I beg you, Cyrano, don't have me arrested. My husband needs me to care for him." She sighed. "The truth is we needed the money to get out of here. My husband works as a carpenter and he was seriously injured on the job. Most of our savings went to pay the doctor for his care. He will be alright, but it will be months before he is well enough to return to work. The problem is, he is too proud to ask for charity. I pick up money here and there as a maid. My fine clothes are hand-me-downs from the rich lady I work for. I started singing in the choirs in hopes that I could become good enough to sing in the cabarets at night. The choir is where I met Emmanuelle. She was the one who convinced me to try and bilk some money out of you. The fifty francs would have paid off our bills and allowed us to travel to his uncle's farm where he could recuperate and finally go back to work."

"And I thought *I* was a good actor," Cyrano mused aloud. "Well, at least I am not out fifty francs. *Madame*, I caution you–do not try this kind of fraud again, or I will aid any other victims in having you put behind bars. You should be forewarned that my father not only works for the royal family, but he is a lawyer, as well. So, I won't press charges...this time. In exchange, you owe me something. An honest answer. Why me?"

Margaux shrugged. "You and your friend seemed well-off and confident. If your family worked for the royals, I reasoned that you wouldn't miss the money, and since you are young and brash, you would get over the heartache quickly. Now, it is your turn to be truthful with *me*–were you really falling in love with me, or with the idea of falling in love?"

The door to #22 opened and a man a few years older than them hobbled to the doorway. "Margaux? What is going on?"

"Nothing, my love. These men are...musketeers...and they are looking for a criminal."

"Well, this neighborhood is full of them. Come back inside."

Margaux turned quickly and whispered to Cyrano. "Please, you must go now, before he suspects something."

"One last thing," Cyrano entreated. "You were very, very convincing when you passionately kissed me. What if I had tried to take it further?"

"Cyrano, I knew that you would never give in to the sin of lust and take advantage of me."

"Really? But how did you know?"

"My dear, a woman *always* knows when she is in the company of a truly chivalrous gentleman. And as for your nose? It gives you...panache."

She turned back to the man in the doorway. "Coming, my love."

Cyrano watched as she walked away for a second, and then suddenly blurted out, "Wait!" He ran up to the door, pulled something from his vest pocket, and gave it to the man. "Here is ten francs...for the information your wife provided. The King's musketeers are grateful for your cooperation."

The man was astonished. "Thank you, Monsieur!"

When Cyrano returned to the cart, Le Bret and D'Artagnan were equally bewildered. "Is everything all right?" Le Bret asked.

"Couldn't be better." Cyrano climbed up on the bench.

"Well...." D'Artagnan leaned across one knee to face the teen. "My keen powers of deduction tell me that your damsel is no longer in distress or you would have called back to us for help, or rather, knowing your temper, you would have barged into that house by yourself to rescue her. So now, my question is this: are *you* alright?"

"I just saved myself a small fortune, and an even bigger embarrassment later, so I am outstanding." Cyrano crossed his arms and legs and looked straight ahead stoically. "Now let's get back to school before they throw us out."

Chapter 46

The biggest problem with being lovelorn wasn't always the pain of rejection. Sometimes, it was because it dulled your awareness of the imminent danger of an even bigger pain.

For a good two weeks, Cyrano moped about school in a dismal fog. He rarely participated in classroom discussions or volunteered answers. On the weekends, when the other freshmen entreated him to venture out into the heart of the city for entertainment, he declined, choosing the seclusion of his room, instead. He didn't even feel like writing or composing poetry.

Le Bret and the others gave him his space, hoping he would eventually come out of it on his own.

Solitude and introspection may have limited spiritual healing powers, but it could prove perilous, as well.

One afternoon, Cyrano was lost in thought and took a wrong turn down one of the hallways in the East Wing that was less traveled. This time, it was completely deserted... until the far end filled with the large shadow of Odo.

Cyrano stopped and suddenly became aware of his surroundings. Instinctively, he looked behind at the other end of the hall. Worse luck. Ruffe and another goonish upperclassman appeared there.

He cursed his carelessness under his breath. He could not imagine a worse situation. Thanks to his sullen mood, not only were his friends not with him, but most likely, none of them knew his whereabouts. He was now surrounded by vengeful enemies and the odds were getting worse all of the time. Antoine De Guiche appeared behind the muscular silhouettes of the other boys.

"Bergerac. Well, well, this is your lucky day." De Guiche sneered smugly. "You're about to get a lesson in humility, and it's all free of charge." He turned his palm up languidly in the same mannerism as his smug, aristocratic father.

"Well, De Guiche, just like your papa, I doubt that you would get your hands dirty in this 'lesson', so that makes it three against one? I hardly call that a fair fight. I think you fellows need to go and get more men."

Odo punched him in the stomach and he doubled over.

"I owe you that one, rich boy."

Cyrano tried to straighten up. "Rich boy?" he pushed out between gasps of air, "At least I don't throw around my old man's wealth ostentatiously, like your master here."

The other older boy punched his chin with a quick jab and then kicked him in his side for good measure when Cyrano went down.

De Guiche leaned over Cyrano's crumpled body. "You *will* learn your place, Bergerac. Underclassmen do not run this place. We do."

If only I had a saber with me, they wouldn't get away with this.

Ruffe stood over him. "I would break your nose, but it looks like someone already beat me to it."

"I fell out of a tree after I conked you good with an apple. What's the excuse with *your* face?" Cyrano got out between more gasps of pain.

De Guiche strode closer to his collapsed body. "One more message for you, Bergerac. Dean Grangier sends his regards."

Ruffe punched him in the face, and the world went black for Cyrano.

* * * *

He woke up on his back many hours later. The ceiling above him was not familiar. When he craned his neck, he realized he was not in the hallway anymore. He was in the college infirmary. With a ringing in his ears. And a splitting headache.

Finally, a recognizable face came into focus. Le Bret loomed over him.

"Hey, *mon ami*, how are you feeling?"

Cyrano blinked repeatedly and managed a wan smile for his friend. "Like my head is in one of the bells up the street at Notre Dame."

"Always with the jokes. Who did this to you?"

"Who do you think? Our ghoulish friends from the stairs."

"We need to tell someone. They can't get away with this."

"No," he grunted as he pulled himself up. "It won't do any good. I have a feeling that was a government-endorsed assassination attempt."

"The Gargoyle?"

"Pretty sure. Now, help me get out of here."

The nurse saw them and bustled over in a dither.

"I'm alright, Sister." Cyrano tried to dismiss her with a wave of his hand. "I just had a clumsy mishap and bumped my head. Haha, silly me."

He smiled, but through his teeth, he muttered to Le Bret, "Get me out of here before I collapse again."

Chapter 47

Once back in their dorm, Le Bret gave Cyrano a long lecture about being low-key and he heeded the advice. He remained unobtrusive for a few weeks, recuperated from his wounds, and tried not to think about revenge.

When the weekend came, Le Bret suggested they go into the heart of town for some relaxation.

"Oh? Is that my reward for being a good little boy?" Cyrano chided.

"Shut up." Le Bret laughed. "You knew these weeks of laying low were for your own good. It's almost the end of the semester. We're practically at the finish line. Now, let's go have some fun."

"All right, but if you don't mind, let me pick out the girls this time. I'd like to find one that is not encumbered with a husband."

The boys decided not to ask the other freshmen to come along. It was time for just best friends. As they strolled along the streets, they joked, laughed, and talked about plans for the Christmas break.

As they stood in the street and debated about where to have lunch, Cyrano caught a glimpse of something far off over Le Bret's shoulder; something glowing in the sunlight. A familiar yellow dress.

He stopped talking to get a better look at the girl in the yellow dress almost a block away. *Is that...? Is that Rox-*

anne?

"Hey, what's the matter with you?" Le Bret called at him impatiently. "You look like you have catalepsy of something."

"I think I just saw Roxanne…."

"Huh? Where?" He followed Cyrano's stare and turned around to a point behind him. "Oh, I see. Well, that can't be Roxanne. Her father would never let her walk the streets of Paris without a duenna."

"Indeed, and instead of a duenna, it looks like she has a male escort." Cyrano fumed.

"What the…oh, *mon dieu*! It looks like Antoine De Guiche is walking with her."

Cyrano would recognize that stupid mop of wavy hair and languorous posture anywhere, "That cad! I must warn Roxanne about that scoundrel." Cyrano's temper was about to explode. He ran after the couple as they headed into a fabric store. The streets were especially crowded for a Saturday afternoon, and he had to evade window shoppers, dodge produce carts, and step over stray animals.

As he turned his head back to yell, "Sorry!" at each one he trampled, he did not look where he was running and nearly bowled over an old woman. "Oh! *Madame*! I am frightfully sorry! I am a clumsy buffoon. Please forgive me." He held her up by both elbows before she spilled onto the sidewalk completely.

The exasperated old matron could not find words, but instead walloped him over the head with her purse.

"Ow! *Madame*! I am not a masher. I'm just a bungler of a boy. Now, if you are not gravely injured, I must excuse myself. It is a matter of great urgency."

Cyrano made it to the doorway of the linen shop without further incident and practically skidded inside.

The surprised proprietor hailed him. "Oh! May I help you, young man?"

He looked about frantically and then gave the shopkeeper a wild look. "Help? Me? Oh! I, uhhh...." He scanned every aisle of the store but did not spy even a glimpse of Roxanne or that scalawag De Guiche.

"Are you looking for any particular material, perhaps for a fine new jacket?"

Finally, he regained his composure and gave a sheepish laugh. "Oh, haha, I was just...looking for my...cousin. Yellow dress? She came in here with an odious-looking young man in a foppish get-up."

"Sorry, I didn't see anyone like that. I might have overlooked them while helping another customer, especially if they were just browsing, as young romantic couples do."

"They're *not* romantic!" He bristled and bolted for the door, then remembered his manners and stuck his head back in the shop. "Thank you!" he yelled, and then disappeared.

He ran to the middle of the intersection and swiveled his head back and forth, maniacally searching for his quarry, but finding no success.

Le Bret caught up with him. "Well, I lost them, and from the savage look on your face, I'd say you weren't any more successful. Better get out of the street before an oxcart flattens you."

"I could swear it was her, Le Bret. How could she fall for that...that vain boor?"

"Relax. It could have been our imagination playing tricks on us."

"On *both* of us? Not likely. Could that primping peacock be the reason she has not responded to my letters? I have to warn her about him."

"Oh, Lord...." Le Bret rolled his eyes.

"Whether she cares for me or not, I am going to have to swallow my foolish pride and go to her address. She needs to know that she is consorting with a wolf in peacock's clothing."

"Yes, of course, *mon ami*. Sounds like a great idea, especially after the great success we had the *last* time we searched for an address for you."

Chapter 48

Le Bret calmed Cyrano and convinced him he should not run right to Roxanne's while this agitated. In fact, he miraculously persuaded him to wait until Sunday—not easy with someone as impetuous as Cyrano.

Roxanne had written down her Paris address for Cyrano before she left *Domaine Bergerac.* This was the one Cyrano was using to send mail to her. Since she hadn't written back, there was always a slight chance that the address was incorrect or old. However, it was the only lead they had and the boys used it to track down the house where she stayed with her aunt, on one of the oldest streets in the city, *Rue Saint Séverin.*

Colleges did not accept female students, something Roxanne hoped to change one day. So the best she could hope for was a menial apprenticeship which would somehow lead to a real writing job someday. She stayed with her aunt because that neighborhood proved closer to the most job opportunities.

The area was on the opposite side of the Seine River from the *College Bauvais.* Without their horses or the musketeer's cart, it turned into a very, very long walk for the boys, one that included the crossing of several bridges. Disregarding the risk of punishment, they skipped out on Sunday mass and left their campus early in the morning. They reached *Rue Saint Séverin* before noon, relieved that the street was nothing like where Margaux lived and looked in fact to be a beautiful neighborhood.

Cyrano found #10 and climbed the steps to the front door ahead of Le Bret. He sighed, rallied his courage, and knocked. After a few seconds, they saw a figure come to the window near the door. Finally, the front door opened and Cyrano gasped in surprise when he saw Roxanne's face.

He started to utter a friendly, sardonic greeting but Roxanne angrily snatched his hat, blurted out "*Baudet*!", and slammed the door in his face.

"What the—?" Cyrano turned back to Le Bret. "D…did she just call me a donkey?"

Le Bret nodded, just as shocked as his friend.

"What did I do? This month is just getting better all the time," Cyrano announced, tone heavy with sarcasm, as he knocked again. "Hey, that's my hat!"

The door quickly swung open again, and Roxanne looked even more furious as she walloped him with the cavalier hat. "I *know* it is! I *gave* it to you!"

"What is *wrong* with you?"

"Over three months! That's how long I have not heard from you!"

"B…but, I've been writing you, sometimes twice a week," he exasperatedly explained. "I haven't gotten any letters from *you*."

Roxanne's eyes smoldered anger as she examined his face. "Are you telling me the truth?"

Cyrano put his fists on his hips. "Now, when is the last time you heard me lie?"

"Hmm, evade, dream, even stretch, but no, never lie…." She stood in the doorway, thinking. "Get in here. Both of you."

She led them to a sitting room in the front of the house,

but everyone being so agitated, no one sat.

"Roxanne," Le Bret started, "I can attest that he wrote many letters to you and you are saying that you wrote to him many times, yet, I can also attest he did not get any from you. Mail service can be inconsistent at times, but it is impossible that all those letters could have been lost. What do you think happened?"

Cyrano shrugged. "I dunno. Is there any chance your duenna could have intercepted them all, mistaking them as improper?"

Roxanne thought for a moment. "That is also impossible. I am sure she was not aware of every time I wrote you a letter. In fact, I don't think I ever asked her to get a courier for me. I always asked someone else."

"Wait, you never summoned a courier yourself?" Cyrano asked.

Roxanne shrugged, too. "No, I'm not that familiar with anyone here yet."

"Then who did you ask? Your aunt? Think!" Le Bret urged.

She gasped, then narrowed her eyes. "My little cousin." She turned her head toward the stairs and bellowed, "*Hugooo!*"

From the sudden clamor of footsteps down the stairs, it seemed to Cyrano that her blood-curdling howl rousted more than one inhabitant of the house. Soon, both Hugo and Aunt Camille rushed into the sitting room.

"*Sacré sang*, Roxanne! What is going on?" a flustered Aunt Camille demanded.

Roxanne ignored her and immediately accosted her dark-haired urchin of a cousin. "Hugo, what did you do with my letters?"

"I gave them to our courier like you told me to." Hugo

recoiled from her disapproving stare.

"You didn't pull a prank, you swear?" she demanded.

"Yes, already!" Hugo had the look of an imp quite capable of such a spoof, but he was clearly intimidated into truthfulness.

Camille crossed her arms. "Dear girl, would you like to enlighten me to your plight?"

"I apologize for my poor manners." Roxanne touched her heart with a dramatic flourish and then pointed an open hand towards the other teens. "Aunt Camille, these are my friends, Henri Le Bret, and my cousin on my father's side—"

"Cyrano de Bergerac," he interrupted and bowed low for the introduction. "If I may.... Hugo, did you use the same courier each time?"

"Yes. There is only one fellow around here with a stout enough horse to make all the trips every few days."

"Ah, and who would that be?"

"Montfleury."

Roxanne clapped her forehead. "Montfleury? Oh, no." She plopped into the chair behind her.

Le Bret crossed his arms. "Hmmm, based on your reaction, Roxanne, I am assuming that Montfleury is particularly unreliable, even inept?"

Roxanne shook her head. "I wish it were just that. Montfleury is a particularly repugnant man where I work. I guess since you never got any of my letters, you don't know this—I got a job in the library at the Sorbonne. I figured that if I can't be a student there, at least I can be around the books and perhaps overhear some writing tips. Anyway, I swear he leers at me constantly through the stacks of books. It makes my skin crawl the way he acts around me. I try not to encourage it, but he is pretty dense. He is not getting the hint. I would not put it past him to intercept all of our letters.

Oh, it gives me the chills thinking about him spying on me."

Cyrano rubbed his chin. "I understand your problem, but at least it was not what I thought."

"What, that I was shunning you?"

"Oh, uh, not that at all!" Cyrano blushed. "I thought that Antoine De Guiche was paying someone to intercept them. Did I see you walking with him yesterday? Roxanne, you must know this—he is a cad and a bully."

She threw head back and guffawed. "Ah-ha-ha-haa!"

"What is so funny?"

"Cyrano, of course I know what Antoine is. He is all that and a pompous, vain imbecile to boot. But he is harmless. This is so funny for *so many* reasons. First, you thought I needed *rescuing*. That's sweet, but funny, nonetheless. I'm not one of the damsels-in-distress from your boyish adventure books. It is also absurd to think that I could be stupid enough to be taken in by someone as shallow as that dullard Antoine." She backhanded his arm.

"Ow! It seems that I am the one in distress…."

"Now here comes the *really* funny part," Roxanne continued. "The only reason I agreed to keep company with him—*platonic* company, mind you—is that when I learned that he was attending *College Bauvais*, I thought I could find out how you were doing and perhaps subtly suggest that he look out for you. So you see, I can't be too angry at you because I guess I thought *you* might need protecting, too. Strange thing, though, when I asked about you, he claimed not to know either of you. Apparently, though, you seem to know *him*…."

"Oh, he knows us, all right; unless he is in the habit of siccing his goons on complete strangers."

"Hmm, so you can add sneaky to his list of qualities, too," Roxanne mused.

"Look," Cyrano started earnestly, "I apologize for not having faith in you, but I didn't hear from you for months, and the next time I see you, you are with my mortal enemy."

"Mortal enemy? I thought maybe your personalities might have clashed; after all, you are everything he is not. But I never thought he would hurt you. I guess I need to apologize to *you*."

"Well, the 'mortal enemy' part was perhaps a bit of hyperbole, but he is not harmless; that is surely no exaggeration."

By this time, Hugo and Aunt Camille had wandered away shaking their heads at the drama that young adults can contrive, and the three friends were left to their typical scheming.

"Now that we are re-united, I have no use for that braying jackass De Guiche. I will be kind and let him down easy, but truth be told, I'm sure he was planning on exploiting me more than I was using him."

"Well, be careful nonetheless when you break the news to him. He can be a very vengeful character," Cyrano warned.

"And so can I. He wouldn't dare harm me or I will threaten to tell every young lady in Paris what a knave he is. Believe me, I can handle him."

Cyrano arched his eyebrows. "Well, far be it from *me* to underestimate you again."

Le Bret added, "You should let us handle your friend Montfleury, though. He sounds like a different reptile altogether."

"Well, as much of a heel as he is, I will not condone you hurting him or poking him with that skewer that you are proudly marching around with," Roxanne reprimanded.

"Oh, sword play? No, nothing as base as that, besides it wouldn't be sporting! I have a much more subtle plan."

The three agreed to meet again the next weekend. The Christmas holiday would be fast approaching after that, and they would make plans to visit each other over the holidays. They also decided that they would find another, more reliable way of corresponding. Finally, they said their goodbyes.

"You know, you broke my white plume when you swatted me with my own hat. I've grown rather fond of that feather," Cyrano chided good-naturedly.

"If you really had forgotten about me after only a few months, that feather is not the only thing I would have broken," Roxanne retorted. "I guess I do owe you a new one."

She kissed him on the cheek. Not the passionate kind of kiss he enjoyed with Margaux, but it was pure and honest. It assured him that their relationship was as sturdy as it ever was, and he would take that.

Chapter 49

On the way back to their college, Cyrano and Le Bret made a detour to the library at the Sorbonne.

The Sorbonne formed part of the University of Paris, one of the oldest colleges in the world. Already over three hundred and fifty years old, it was home to one of the greatest libraries in existence, including a legal library.

"Now, what's the plan again, Cyrano?"

"We are two legal clerks for a very, very, important barrister here in Paris, and whatever you do, don't let him actually see the text of any of the books we use."

"Got it."

Armed with a detailed description of what Montfleury looked like (a squat, chubby man with bad hygiene who obsessively mopped his sweaty brow), Cyrano and Le Bret assumed their characters and strolled into the library to hatch a devious, seventeenth-century-style practical joke.

Cyrano found Montfleury behind a help desk at the library and addressed him in a comical accent to disguise his own Gascon origins. "Excuse me, where can I find your legal volumes?"

Montfleury eyed him with skepticism. "*You* want legal books?"

"Yes, I'm interning for the law firm of *Étouffant, Fanfaronnades, and Soufflet* and they sent me, and my associate here, to do some research on a case. Is there something funny about that?" Cyrano feigned impatience.

"No, no, of course not. It's just that…never mind. Follow me."

Just as Cyrano had hoped, all of the legal volumes were housed in a private room, and Montfleury stayed with them suspiciously instead of excusing himself.

"Henri, we must begin our search with the most recent citations. Look for volumes that recorded royal high court cases from last year…."

The two pretended to search the volumes until Cyrano settled on a single tome, set in on a reading table, and paged through it furiously.

"Ah! Here it is, my friend. Oh my! According to this ruling, the boss' new client is really in for it. They ruled against this fellow for the same thing and he was severely punished. All that for stealing someone's mail. Tsk, tsk."

Montfleury could not help but hear him and the trap lay set. "What's that? What are you talking about?" he demanded as he craned over Cyrano's shoulder.

Cyrano quickly turned away from Montfleury's prying eyes, cradling the book with him, pacing back and forth as he pretended to read. "Yes, yes, yes. The poor beggar! How about that? I thought they saved burning at the stake for witches. Ah, well, I'm not sure we can help this one. The judges in Paris are particularly harsh. He will be fricasseed by the end of the week…."

"For taking mail?" Montfleury hopped after him.

"Oh, look, *mon ami*!" Le Bret's turn now, pointing at the contents of another volume. "This one was just eight months ago, establishing a legal precedent here in the city. This unfortunate stooge was convicted of publicly leering at a young woman *and* stealing her correspondence. They showed no mercy on him at all."

Montfleury gulped. "Really? What did they do to him?"

"They publicly whipped him and *then* they burned him at the stake! *Quelle honte!*"

"I didn't read anything about that. Surely, I would have remembered—" Montfleury began nervously.

"Oh, yes! *I* remember hearing about that." Cyrano interrupted. "It was too gruesome to be reported in the newspapers. And I believe the judge was so angry he forbade anyone to speak the man's name again!"

"No!" Le Bret slammed his volume closed in pretend shock.

"Yes!" Cyrano hurriedly slammed his book closed in reply and put it back onto the shelf. "Well, it's all there in black and white. Quickly, we must return to the boss' study to report our findings. Oh, I don't envy our client one bit. I hope he has his last will and testament in order."

"Well, if he doesn't, I am sure the boss can take care of that, too, haha. I'd better tell him to get paid in advance, though." Le Bret added for good measure.

Cyrano turned to the pale-faced Montfleury and bowed officiously. "Thank you for your help, *Monsieur*. I only wish we could have discovered more hopeful news for our client." He brought his face down close to Montfleury's and examined him for a second. "Say friend, you don't look too well. Perhaps you should see a physician, or at least go home."

Montfleury steadied himself on a chair back. "Yes, I am feeling a bit…dizzy…right now."

"Hmm, could be a case of the Dropsy," Le Bret offered. "Cheer up, though, old man, it could be worse. You could be our mail thief client who'll be getting seared like a rack of lamb. Ha, ha."

"Wait!" Montfleury gasped after them, "Your boss, is he available for hire?"

"Why?" Cyrano turned back to him, "are you in some manner of trouble?"

"Ahh, er, perhaps…"

"Well, my friend, if it is anything close to the same kind of trouble as our present client, I have but one piece of free legal advice for you: flee! Leave the city as soon as possible and never return. Go become a traveling actor or some other disreputable vocation. *Adieu*!"

Cyrano and Le Bret stumbled out of the Sorbonne library chuckling to themselves. The last they saw of Montfleury, he was clutching his chest and looking about wildly.

"Ha, ha. Well, I don't think he will be bothering Roxanne for quite some time."

"You are right. I am still laughing, thinking about the look of terror on his face. At least it will make the long, cold walk back to school tolerable."

Chapter 50

The last week before the Christmas holiday at *College Bauvais* proved to be a bustling, busy one. All of the students nervously prepared for final assessments of some sort—final exams, final papers, or final recitations.

Cyrano was not as anxious as most freshmen. As expected, he and Le Bret fared quite well during their first, mid-year finals week. Le Bret took an elective in Art and received highest honors for his drawings, prompting many to say that perhaps one day, the Cardinal would admire his work and buy it for the Royal Collection.

The finals for Science and Literature happened earlier in the week and, as expected, Cyrano received top honors for those classes.

Today brought finals in Math and Theology. Both boys felt they had fared pretty well and passed for the term, but they really didn't care if they received honors for those areas of study.

Tomorrow would be the final in Rhetoric class. Cyrano could not care less about his final assessment for The Gargoyle. Due to his keen mind and nimble tongue, Grangier could find no way to fail him without raising the suspicions of The Provost.

Unbeknownst to Cyrano, The Provost had made it known to the faculty that Cyrano was literally a protégé, but he was not worried about Grangier's final grade.

All he needed to do tomorrow was write a typical response to a few test questions. *Here is proposition 'A'. Support or refute the main argument of the proposition.* Simple for Cyrano, a master at winning arguments.

What he was really focused on was his Drama final on Friday, the last day before the break. Not a paper and pencil test of knowledge of Drama or theater terms; instead, it would be a performance-based final. Every freshman had to go on stage by themselves and recite something that would take about five minutes—an oration, a famous speech, a soliloquy from a play or a poem.

Cyrano did not worry that he wouldn't do well; far from it. He relished the undivided attention he received on stage and performing came like second nature to him. He knew he would do well, but he wanted to be perfect. He wanted to be remembered for this performance the same way he was remembered for standing up to the *Marquis* in the bakery; the same way he was remembered for winning the fencing competition; the same way he was remembered for taking on Grangier.

Since re-kindling his relationship with Roxanne, he became inspired. He felt like writing verses again. For his performance at the Drama finals, he would recite his own work of poetry, but it would have to be his masterpiece.

Like so many times since arriving at school, Cyrano used his room to concentrate and summon his creativity. It turned into his refuge where he could shut out all the distractions, avoid the negative energy, free his mind, and produce his craft. It was the closest thing he had to sitting under his favorite tree at *Domaine Bergerac*.

Roxanne became once again his heart's desire and therefore his muse. He knew that the topic of his brainchild would have to be about his longing for romantic love. It consumed his waking thoughts almost as much as his obsession for joining the musketeers.

His work would be a love sonnet.

All he needed now was the right inspiration. He closed his eyes, envisioned Roxanne's breathtaking face before him, and imagined he was saying everything he ever wanted to say to her. After a few moments, he opened his eyes, found his paper, and started to write.

Once he began, he found he could not stop. It poured out of him, not like a fountain, not like a well, but more like the raging waters of a waterfall.

An hour later, he knew he would not need a second night to work on the sonnet. In fact, he would not need another minute. In his mind, he'd attained the perfection he had been seeking.

By this time, it had turned into a dark, wintry night. Le Bret would be back in the room soon for curfew. Cyrano was already exhausted from his writing and as anxious as he was to get Le Bret's opinion, he didn't feel like waiting another moment for him. He pulled the thick curtains closed to ward off the chilly draft from the windows, doused the lanterns in the room, and stumbled off to a satisfied sleep.

Chapter 51

The next day, Cyrano and Le Bret grappled their way through Rhetoric finals like a marathon runner staggering his way through the finish line.

As relieved as he was about getting that over with, Cyrano knew that his real relief would come tomorrow after he delivered his stage performance and received his accolades in Drama. Despite thinking ahead to that moment, he could not shake the strange, uneasy feeling that Grangier was staring at him during the entire exam period. *He probably thinks I am cheating or something and wants to try and nab me in the act. Ugh! I guess that icy stare is another reason they call him* The Gargoyle.

That evening, Cyrano and Le Bret packed their travel bags for the Christmas break. A coach would be picking them up—like most students—immediately after school dismissal so they could take advantage of the remaining hours of daylight for the trip home.

He could not think of a better scenario to finish the semester tomorrow. The day would end with Drama class, and he would be the last student to perform on stage. He would dazzle his professors and peers with his impeccable delivery of the sonnet; school would dismiss, everyone would be talking about him, and he would leave for Christmas at home with the accolades still ringing in his ears.

Friday did not go exactly as planned for him.

Chapter 52

Many of the boys started Friday morning by saying their goodbyes, particularly those who would not see each other in class later in the day. This was especially true of upper-classmen who had taken some first years under their wing.

"Well, pups, I guess I won't see you again until after the New Year." Lucien bid adieu to his charges.

"Dupont, thank you for all of your advice and guidance," Le Bret acknowledged.

"Yes, our deepest gratitude," Cyrano added. "But why wait until January? Come visit me at *Domaine Bergerac* after Christmas. Le Bret will be there, as well."

Lucien shook his head. "My family owns several farms and the parsnips need to be stored soon. Father thinks it will be a good experience for me to oversee the harvest."

"Ha, well, I'm sure you will make a fine Lord of the Manor."

The boys started walking away from each other and towards their last day of classes.

"Hmm, well, I'd much rather be a politician than a farmer, but even Cato and Cincinnatus had to start somewhere. Oh, and Cyrano? One last piece of advice," Lucien called after them.

The boys stopped and walked back to Lucien when they saw the look of concern on his face.

"Oh, it's probably nothing…but there's been some

strange whispering among the upperclassmen about a freshman who might be 'getting what's coming to him'. Nonsense, I'm sure, but just be careful."

Cyrano patted him on the shoulder. "You're right, it's probably nothing; but thanks for the warning, nonetheless."

Le Bret turned to Cyrano as they strode off to *Salon St. Hubert*. "Well, what do you make of that? Lucien knows *every*thing that goes on at this school. That could be a credible threat."

He avoided Le Bret's concerned gaze and continued on. "Piffle! Stop worrying like an old mother hen. You are starting to sound like Yvette. Next, you'll want to wipe the snot off my big nose."

"It wouldn't hurt not to make so many enemies. The list is getting longer."

"Then my honor grows as well." Cyrano smiled grimly. "Besides, nothing can spoil my day today."

Like so many other days of the semester, the boys slogged through their schedule. With finals mostly over, the professors lauded praise for those who excelled and aimed portentous warnings for those who habitually slacked.

Nobody cared about scholarly doom and gloom. The time had come to exhale and socialize. Being a freshman meant that you were at a peculiar age. No longer a boy, but not considered a man by a fair piece of society, unless you were king. As such, a lot of the first years talked about Christmas like they were children. All of them spoke fondly about being home with their families and enjoying their traditions.

Cyrano happily tried to join the frivolity, but his ego kept on distracting him. He was focused on the afternoon when he would be on the stage performing. In his own arrogant imagination, he saw his professor lauding him as a prodigy and his reputation among his peers as a well-rounded polymath would be cemented. He only wished Roxanne could be there to listen to him, too. If she swooned at his romantic rhymes, perhaps he would be brave enough to tell her she was the inspiration for them, and he might even seize the opportunity to profess his undying love.

Cyrano noticed that Le Bret was being feted as well for his artistic talents, and he was glad for him. But throughout the remainder of the day, he got the lion's share of praise. Professors like Sorel and Gauthier fed his already robust pride by recognizing his giftedness in science and literature. Back at his small, county cloister school, Cyrano was a big, precocious, fish in a small pond. He longed to be the whale of the seven seas, and now that he was getting that attention he craved, he was gobbling it up and greedy for one more dessert.

As they say, though, pride goeth before a fall.

Chapter 53

Antoine De Guiche called a meeting in his dorm room. Ruffe, Odo, and six other upper-class lummoxes were in attendance. With the merriment of the last day of the term, no one missed their sinister faces.

"So, are you all clear about the plan?" De Guiche asked for confirmation.

"Uh-huh," Odo assented dully. "Franck will take care of his friend Le Bret, Gustave will distract Professor Picard, Roger will guard the stage entrance in case anyone wants to try and be a hero and help him."

"And then what?" Antoine quizzed.

Ruffe continued. "That will leave me, Odo, and the others to take on Big Nose and soften him up."

"So I can have the honor of landing the final assault," Antoine concluded with glee. "Everyone understand—I must be the one who finishes him off! Do your job, and I will make sure that all of you enjoy a rich Christmas bounty."

"I just don't get one part of the plan, Boss. Why do we need seven guys to take him on?" Odo wondered.

"Idiot! Have you ever seen him fence? When he is at full strength, he can beat the best in school. He could probably take on two or three weaker fencers at the same time. So, we need to tip the scales heavily in our favor. Once we get that little braggart out of the way, all of the underclassmen will fear us again and we will control the whole school."

"But Boss, what about the rest of the faculty? Won't we be expelled once they find out that we ganged up on a single freshman?"

"We will leave that to Grangier. He will testify, as will all of you, that Big Nose attacked me first and that I had no choice but to defend myself. Thankfully, *The Gargoyle* has as much of a score to settle with him as I do. Now, we have about an hour before Big Nose is due to appear in the auditorium. So, get to your posts now so that you will be waiting backstage for him before he even gets there."

While the rest of them filed out of his room, Ruffe and Odo remained behind at De Guiche's request.

"This seems like a wickedly good plan, Boss." Ruffe wrung his hands in delight. "Do you think that we'll be able to hurt Big Nose enough that he won't want to come back to school next semester?"

"Hurt him?" De Guiche laughed with delight. "Hahaha, you idiot! I plan to kill him! Use your head. If he remains alive, he could eventually convince everyone that we ambushed him. Have you not heard about his antics in Rhetoric class? Even Grangier can't win a legal argument against that snot! No, the only way for us to get away with this is if he is no longer alive to refute my self-defense alibi."

"*Mon Dieu!*" Odo gasped.

"Ohhh, don't go soft on me now, you lunk-head! Death is what that impudent loud-mouth deserves; especially for foiling my plans to seduce that luscious redhead. Hmm, with him out of the way, I might just win her back."

"Do you think she might have a friend for me?" Ruffe asked hopefully.

"Hahaha. Well, I don't know about that, but you oafs are welcome to plunder her duenna. Now get out of here!"

Chapter 54

Drama class finally commenced. Cyrano waited impatiently as each one of his classmates preceded him on the stage and gave their various monologues, odes, and soliloquies. He tried to be courteous, clapping politely for each one of his colleagues, no matter how mundane or banal he found their performances.

He had easily committed the poem to memory so he was not anxious about flubbing his lines, but he bounced in his seat nonetheless as his friends recited poems by John Donne and William Shakespeare.

"Stop it," Le Bret chastised. "You look like you are galloping on *Storm*."

"All right, all right," Cyrano conceded. "I just can't wait to be done."

"Oh, come on! Don't lie to me. If you wanted this over with, you would have jumped up first. You just can't wait for the acclaim."

"True." He smiled sheepishly. "Do me a favor? Go backstage and make sure there are extra lanterns. I want the lighting on stage to be just right."

Le Bret got up and smiled back at him as he headed towards the stage door. "Attention hog!"

Backstage looked dark. Le Bret could hear Gérard reciting a Ronsard ode.

Sweetheart, let's see if the rose

That this morning had open
Her crimson dress to the Sun,
This evening hasn't lost
The folds of her crimson dress,
And her complexion similar to yours…

Le Bret fumbled around in the dark, but he did not find a lantern or candle. Instead, he found a rather large, surly upperclassman; the one that, unfortunately, was looking for him.

The goon grabbed Le Bret by the lapel and slammed him into a wall. The stunned victim offered little resistance and the older boy dragged him towards a closet. As he threw him in, Le Bret banged his head into the back wall and blacked out. The upperclassmen propped a chair and several sandbags against the door to lock him in, just in case he came to before they jumped Cyrano.

On stage, Gérard came to the conclusion of the ode.

So if you believe me, my sweetheart,
While time still flowers for you,
In its freshest novelty,
Do take advantage of your youthful bloom:
As it did to this flower, the doom
Of age will blight your beauty.

Cyrano breathed a sigh of relief as Professor Picard rose from the front row of the auditorium and spoke.

"Thank you, Gérard, a fine choice. A classic piece from the leader of a group of noble poets called the Pleiads. Just a few historic notes about the Pleiads before we conclude the day with our final performance…."

At that, Cyrano headed for the stage door with the lantern he was going to use as a prop.

Out of the corner of his eye, he spied a familiar wisp of red hair escaping from the otherwise-perfect coif of a person in the front row. *Was that a girl?*

Mon Dieu, are my eyes playing tricks on me again? Could it be, could it be...Roxanne?

He had to know if he was going mad, or if his dream had just come true.

"Roxanne," he whispered over to the girl. "Roxanne, is that you?"

"Shhh!" the female figure responded and came over to him.

It *was* her.

"Roxanne! What are you doing here? If I knew that this recitation were open to the public, I would have surely invited you. I never even knew that they would allow women in here."

"Again, shhh! I am here for my new job. I am reporting for *The Gazette*. Isn't that wonderful? I am indeed the only woman here. That's why I want to keep it quiet. I need to prove to my publisher that a woman can handle this kind of work."

"Hmm, I understand. The last thing you need is this pack of wolves howling at you."

"So, are you on stage next? I guess so, since the professor said the final performance."

"Indeed, I am next."

"Good luck!" She squeezed his arm.

It gave him even more incentive to shine on stage.

Fortune stuck close to Cyrano as he entered the backstage area. He knew it would dark back there and he used his lantern to find his way. It helped him see that something wasn't quite right. His lantern light fell upon Ruffe, Odo, and few other upperclassmen.

Uh-oh, this could be bad....

"Excuse me, gentlemen," he declared with typical bravado. "But I'm afraid you have the wrong night. The circus isn't due to perform here until next week."

Ruffe narrowed his eyes at the insult and threw a punch at Cyrano's stomach. He narrowly dodged the roundhouse strike and countered by swinging his lantern, clopping Ruffe on the chin. Sparks flew everywhere.

Cyrano's self-satisfaction caught up with him as he did not notice Odo sneaking up from behind until he landed a powerful jab to his kidneys. He buckled to the ground but did not black out.

Odo stood over him, laughing. "Where's your smart mouth now, *Gascon*?"

Cyrano gulped down bile as he heard Professor Picard's voice.

"And now for the last performance of the afternoon, and the semester, Monsieur Cyrano de Bergerac will recite his own composition, a romantic sonnet."

He found his hat in the dark, and with his head still down, he rushed at Odo and rammed into his stomach, knocking the wind out of him.

Cyrano turned right, ran, and skidded onto the stage. Still out of breath, he composed himself quickly, dusted off his hat, gave a quick bow, and started the recital.

I was enslaved to unquenched thirst
I traversed this world to find redress...
Was I doomed to life coerced,
A hopeless quest for happiness?

He became too engrossed in performing and forgot the danger. He wandered too far over to the other side of the stage, and two more of De Guiche's thugs grabbed him and pulled him into the wings. One grabbed him from behind and locked his arms while the other used a large, wooden belaying pin to land a few strikes to his ribcage. Cyrano used the heels of his boots to stomp on his captor's insteps. That loosened the grip on his arms just enough for him to escape and get back on stage.

His pride would not allow him to tell the audience of the attacks or plead for help. Instead, he continued with the sonnet as if he had just forgotten something offstage.

I chased Eratos' face in vain
It left me longing, empty hearted...
Haunted by the specter of pain
Nightmares of a love departed....

Cyrano tried to avoid another ambush by keeping to the center of the stage and away from the wings, but once again, he was too concerned with being the focus of attention. He wandered too far upstage towards the backdrop curtains, where two more older boys waited for him. They pulled him behind the curtain and tried to wrap a rope around his midsection in an attempt to hoist him up like a punching bag.

Using the skills honed from tree-climbing, Cyrano grabbed the rope higher up and kicked his feet towards the back brick wall of the stage. He scaled the wall like a mountain climber to escape from his attackers. When he had almost reached the ceiling, he looped a length of the rope around the battens and the joists and rappelled back down to kick his foes in the head, like a true swashbuckler. Back on the ground, with his enemies temporarily subdued, he dove out from behind the backdrop and continued his monologue as if nothing happened.

I was lost, but came my salvation
A sweet face appeared above...
And gave my soul restoration
Such is the promise of Love...

Professor Picard peevishly called from the first row of the house. "*Monsieur* Cyrano, the assignment called for you to memorize your entire poem. Are you checking your lines offstage?"

"Certainly not, sir! I was ah, em, checking the time to make sure I did not go over."

"Do not fret about that. I will let you know if you are in danger. You have ten more seconds."

"Ah, capital, as I am at the closing couplet."

It is providence no more, no less
Our love is sacred, heaven bless'd....

Cyrano was hoping to bask in applause, but he took a glimpse towards the wings off of stage left and saw that Antoine De Guiche had joined the six older boys. They had Le Bret in their clutches, a rope around his neck. They quietly shook their fists, taunted him, and pantomimed threats to Le Bret's person if Cyrano did not surrender to them.

Rage filled him. His body quaked with anger and he no longer cared about the limelight or applause; just revenge. He broke into a dead run, picked up speed, and launched himself at the boys. A bloodcurdling battle cry rose from his throat as he leaped high into the air and jumped into the pile of bodies.

While the group of goons wrestled with Cyrano and Le Bret, De Guiche seized the opportunity to frame Cyrano and cement his alibi. He staggered out behind the curtain just far enough to get the attention of Grangier and Picard. "He is a madman! Cyrano De Bergerac is attacking people backstage! He is assaulting me personally!"

De Guiche dramatically staggered back towards the wings where the boys were pummeling Cyrano. "That's enough," he ordered. "Ruffe, Odo, hold him up. The rest of you, get out of here before you get caught. And take Le Bret with you. Now go!"

Once the others were gone, Antoine turned away from

Cyrano for a moment and unsheathed a saber that was at his side. He turned back around to face him with a malevolent smile.

"Well, *Gascon*, you are finally about to get yours. I'm not sure what I'm going to enjoy more—running you through with this blade, or consoling that redheaded cupcake of yours when you are gone."

Cyrano choked back his anger and calmly chided his tormentor. "So, this is your idea of a fair fight? You gutless cur! Seven against one? And now you are going to kill an unarmed man? Roxanne will know what a coward you are, if she doesn't already. My grandfather was right. You and your kin will never know the meaning of the word 'honor'."

Le Bret had no idea where they were taking him, but he overheard what De Guiche said as he was being led away. In his mind, he thought this could be the end for both he and Cyrano, and decided on one last act of desperation.

On their way out, he kicked over one of the few lit lanterns backstage. It sent oil and sparks everywhere. His captors panicked and let go of him to reach for blankets and water pails that were kept around for just such an emergency.

In the ensuing confusion, Cyrano backed his way onto center stage. "If you are going to kill me, I'm at least going to make sure there are witnesses," he yelled loud enough for the audience to hear and opened his hands so that all could see he was unarmed.

Le Bret ran from his would-be kidnappers and burst out of the side stage door and into the audience. He started to search for Professor Picard in the dark to warn him of Cyrano's impending doom, but then had a better idea. Picard wanted a large audience for his freshman performers and the Provost thought the entire student body might be entertained by the recital, so everyone was there, including Roberte.

Le Bret called out to him. "Roberte! Are you near the stage?"

"Yes, I am." He stood up. "Why?"

He ran towards Roberte. "Do you have your saber with you?"

"No, only my épée. My saber is packed."

"It will have to do. Quickly!" He gestured towards the stage, and Roberte understood.

"Here, Cyrano! I believe you could use this." Raul tossed the épée onto the stage.

Cyrano picked it up and saluted him with his own sword. "Much obliged."

He turned towards De Guiche in the wings and beckoned him onto the stage. "It's now more of a fair fight, my dear Antoine. Well, perhaps it would be if I tied one hand behind my back."

De Guiche no longer cared about discretion and angrily ran at Cyrano and tried to plunge his saber into his torso in full view of the entire faculty and student body.

Cyrano deftly parried the lunge safely away from him, and De Guiche stumbled past. Several students tried to rush the stage and come to Cyrano's aid, but he held up a hand to stop them. He even shooed them back with a wave. He then turned towards De Guiche again. He could not help himself and he mocked the clumsy attempt at killing him.

"I think you missed. But I had a thought, Antoine. I have an even better way of making this a fair fight while simultaneously completing my drama assignment, *and* keeping the audience entertained, as well. I will compose another sonnet while I fight you. Hmm, just a moment while I think…ah, I have it!"

I applaud you, sir, you've made me mad
So I toss aside the cape I'm clad

He made a big show of unclasping his cloak and tossing it out to the audience.

I shall duel you while I compose a poem
And at the end, I will strike home

Cyrano motioned at De Guiche, inviting him to attack again, and Antoine made another inept charge. He swatted it aside without breaking his own stride. As De Guiche recovered, the two of them circled around each other, and Cyrano continued to rhyme.

You strut just like a bird of spring
But watch out, robin, I'll clip your wing
You preen as if you have a coxcomb
But at the end, I will strike home

At the end of each line, he punctuated it by flicking the épée at De Guiche and slashing a sleeve here, severing a button there.

I'll be direct, I shall not tarry
My last attack you will not parry
It's as plain and bald as Grangier's dome
That at the end, I will strike home

"Ruffe! Odo! Where are you?" De Guiche hissed, but this time, his henchmen did not come to his aid.

The enraged De Guiche mounted another attack, but Cyrano calmly fended off each swipe in a ringing cacophony that fencers call a "Conversation." Cyrano led him around the stage like an expert matador working the ring and wearing down the bull for the final thrust. *Don Diego would be proud of this metaphor. Olé! Ah, well, back to my stanza....*

In your distress, your cronies you call
But even they cannot break your fall
You hide and cower just like a gnome
But all in vain, I will strike home

The exhausted De Guiche tried one last feeble onslaught, but Cyrano caught the hilt of the saber with the fat part of the épée and, in a whirling circular motion called an envelopment, dislodged the weapon from Antoine's grasp. It flew high into the 'flies' of the stage. Cyrano caught it deftly as it came down.

I seize your sword; you will not keep her
Sad? Be thankful you don't meet the Reaper
I may not plant you in the loam
But nonetheless, I will strike home

He nonchalantly strutted towards De Guiche, whipped his sword at Antoine's boots, and swept his feet out from under him. He splayed onto the floor of the stage.

The finale has come and I prevail
And you, the bully, again will fail

De Guiche realized the horror of his situation. He'd failed to kill Cyrano, he was disarmed, on the ground, and his enemy was coming at him with a sword. Hundreds of witnesses saw him attack Cyrano so they would not blame him for retaliating. He turned over and desperately started crawling on all fours to get away from him. Tears of anger and embarrassment stung his eyes.

Tell all of Paris, even Rome
It is the end, and I strike… home

On the last word, Cyrano jabbed the épée into De Guiche's butt cheek. De Guiche yelped in pain and scrambled off of the stage into the waiting arms of several large faculty members.

Half of the audience gasped, and the other half cheered with delight.

Oh, well, I am going to probably get expelled for this stunt, anyway, so I might as well bask in this moment… Cyrano thought as he bowed ostentatiously to the crowd.

He hopped off the stage. Numerous underclassmen

clapped him on the back. He never got tired of their adulations. He checked on Le Bret first. "Are you alright?"

Le Bret nodded. "I'm fine, but that's the closest I ever want to come to being garroted."

Cyrano moved on through the auditorium to reach a stern-faced Roxanne, "Uh-oh, am I in trouble again?" He hoped humor would break her mood.

"You could have been killed...and I would have died from melancholy!" Roxanne scolded. Her expression changed to great relief and she hugged him so tightly that her strength shocked him.

It's nice to know you care...Wait! She cares for me!

"Yes, but think of what a sensational story it would have made for *The Gazette*," he retorted with typical self-deprecation.

Roxanne laughed. "I can't stay mad at you. I can see now how dangerous Antoine is; you were just defending yourself, and he certainly deserves a sharp pain in the *derrière*."

Cyrano laughed back at her characteristic bawdiness. "Well, you don't have to worry any more. One way or another, I don't think De Guiche and I will be in each other's company again."

"Hmm, that sounded cryptic, my dear. You will have to excuse me while I interview more of the audience for my story, but when I am done, I'm coming back for an explanation."

"Go. Be a good journalist." He smiled at her.

"Cyrano!"

The voice of the Provost came from the other side of the auditorium. He could see the official walking briskly towards him, with a rather officious-looking military man matching his stride. His smile vanished.

Uh-oh, here it comes. Mon Dieu! *Am I in that much*

trouble that he had to call the Paris Guard *on me? I thought I was just going to be expelled, not clapped in irons. Oh, well, if Father could spring Don Diego out of jail, I should be— What the—?* Don Diego*?? Am I hallucinating? Is that Don Diego behind them?*

Presently, they were upon him, and the Provost spoke up first. "Cyrano, I can officially say that the *College* is not where you belong...."

His heart sank, but he was prepared for his fate.

The Provost continued. "I would like to introduce you to *Capitaine* Claude Carbon."

"I see. Well, it a pleasure to make your acquaintance, *Capitaine*. Will you be immediately whisking me away to a moldy dungeon, or can I clean myself up first?"

Carbon cleared his throat. "Well, our garrison is not exactly the Royal Palace, but I would hardly call it a dungeon."

"I...I don't understand?" Cyrano looked at each face quizzically.

It was indeed Don Diego's face that he saw behind them, and now he excitedly jumped into the conversation. "Master Cyrano, as a little surprise, I asked your father if I could take his coach to pick up you and Le Bret for the Christmas holiday. In my eagerness, I arrived quite early, and your Provost invited me to the auditorium to watch you perform. That is where I met my new friend here, *Capitaine* Carbon. I could not help but brag about how I tutored you and what a great swordsman you are, and well, he just witnessed that I was not exaggerating."

Cyrano's mind was reeling. Here was his friend and mentor, a Spaniard, rubbing elbows with a French Army officer that may have once been on the other side of a battlefield, and conversing about...him. Apparently, from living with Grandfather, Diego's French was getting better. Cyrano decided not to let the details of his nationality slip out, just in case it had not yet come up in polite conversation.

"Indeed," Carbon added, startling Cyrano out of his musings. "I am *Capitaine* of the *Gascon Guard*. May I ask when your eighteenth birthday is?"

"Er, in little more than two months."

"Close enough. I would like to offer you a commission in my regiment. I could use more fearless, talented cadets like you."

"So, I'm not expelled, and I'm not going to jail?"

The Provost let out a bellowing laugh. "I forgot to tell you, Carbon, that he has an incredible sense of humor, as well."

Cyrano was overwhelmed and uncharacteristically silent as he processed these unfolding events. He was being offered an opportunity for military duty. It wasn't his dream of being in the vaunted Musketeers, but it represented a chance at excitement, glory, and yes, even danger. It might even eventually lead to an opening with the Musketeers. *Should I take it?*

Just then, Le Bret came bounding up to them, huffing and out of breath. "Ah…there you are! Provost, I am a witness. I can attest that De Guiche ambushed Cyrano and tried to make it look like he was the aggressor."

"Thank you, Le Bret," the Provost replied politely. "But I believe that it is already apparent to everyone at the *College*, with perhaps the exception of Professor Grangier, that Cyrano was in the right."

It was then that Cyrano knew his path and what his decision would be.

"*Capitaine* Carbon, I will happily accept your commission with the Guard on two conditions. One, that I be able to go home for Christmas and say my goodbyes to my family.

And two, that my friend here, Le Bret, be offered a commission as well."

"Hmm, well, a package deal," Carbon mused aloud, and then offered a handshake to Cyrano. "I do believe that both can be arranged."

"Huh? What did I miss? Am I missing something here?" A bewildered Le Bret shook Carbon's hand, as well.

"I'll explain it all to you on the way to *Domaine Bergerac*. Come, let's collect Roxanne and give her a ride home, as well. I believe she has a publishing deadline to meet."

The boys saluted Carbon, thanked the Provost, and continued their farewells to their classmates.

As they brought Roxanne back to her aunt's house, Cyrano delicately explained that everything was well, that he was not in any trouble, but he had some decisions to make. He asked that Roxanne come to *Domaine Bergerac* the day after Christmas and he would explain everything to her.

Chapter 55

Christmas at *Domaine Bergerac* that year was especially festive and memorable. The gifts were grand, the food grander, and the affections most frank and candid.

Abel took the news about school and the Guard surprisingly well and did not bluster about it. Mama was understandably emotional about her baby joining a regiment, but even she came around.

Savignion and Don Diego were especially proud and excited for him. Even if he never faced the harsh realities of battle—and they hoped he never had to—he had brought honor upon himself and his kin.

The grimness of his own decision was not lost on Cyrano. As cavalier as he was during times of crisis, he knew that joining the *Gascon Guard* may someday put his life in great peril. France was a great and proud nation. That patriotism could lead them to war with their neighbors—Spain, England, even Prussia or Italy—at a moment's notice. War. Death. The end. No more days of summer. No more hopes of love or kisses. No more time with Roxanne.

Roxanne!

The thought of her tore at him. He was truly at a crossroads in his life. One path led to potential adventure and glory, the things he always longed for; the other path offered a possible life with Roxanne, something he craved just as much.

The debate raged in him all that December 26th. Roxanne was coming that night and he would have to tell her. Tell her *something*. Finally, he knew what.

From a young age, Cyrano felt that he had a destiny for an exceptional existence. In the last year, many people had stepped into his life and confirmed his feelings. He wanted both glory and happiness with Roxanne, but there was only one thing to do: compromise now and hopefully have both one day. He was confident she cared for him. She didn't come right out and profess her love, but he somehow knew it and that was enough, for now. The problem was, should he reveal his love to her?

He toyed with the idea of asking her to marry him. *Lots of people our age get married. Royals do it all the time. We could wed quickly. Elope. Find a priest, and be united before I have to leave for the military.*

Finally, sadly, he concluded it would not be fair to Roxanne. *What if war broke out? What if I died in battle? She admitted that if Antoine had succeeded in killing me, she would be heartsick. How much more so if she were to become a widow at such a young age? I cannot do that to someone I love so much!*

He vowed not to reveal his true love to her when she came that night. If they were meant to be together, it would happen when he was done serving his country.

Dinner that night would include not only Papa and Mama, but Professor Gassendi—who was now officially courting Yvette, *Grandfather*, Don Diego, and of course, Roxanne.

Finally, the moment arrived, and Roxanne walked through the door of the *château* in time for dinner. They were elated to see each other, but Cyrano became quiet and somber during the meal.

Afterwards, Roxanne took his hand and led him away from the table. "You are so glum! Don't you want me here?"

"Are you insane? Of course I want you here. It's just that…" He heaved a gigantic sigh. "It's time to deliver my news."

"Hmm, I think I'd better sit down for this." She led him to his parlor and they sat.

Cyrano could not stand the sadness any longer so he lightened the mood one last time with his infamous brand of humor. "Very well. Since you will become a famous journalist, I thought I would deliver my news in your preferred style. This is Cyrano's gazette: Monday, December 26 in the year of our Lord 1633. Many Christmas revelers did not return to work and continued to celebrate. Madeleine de Robineau, also known to her beloved friends as Roxanne, visited *Domaine Bergerac* where she was welcome and feted for her exploits as a great female writer. Henri Le Bret is expected at the same residence tomorrow and three great friends will be reunited for an unfortunately short while. In other related news, Hercule-Savinien Cyrano De Bergerac, along with his friend, the above-mentioned Le Bret, have accepted commissions to become cadets in the storied regiment of the *Gascon Guard*—"

Roxanne gasped loudly and stared at him for several interminable moments. She said not a word but wrapped her arms around his neck tightly, buried her face in his shoulder, and sobbed loudly. After what seemed like five minutes, she composed herself, but she still did not speak. She rose and ran upstairs to the guest room. Cyrano could hear the door slam.

The rest of the family ran in to the sitting room to see what the commotion was, but the lump in his throat made it impossible to talk. After a few moments, he felt fatigue overtake him and he retired upstairs to his own room for one last night of fitful sleep in his own bed. He thought about knocking on Roxanne's door, but he could not compel his body to do so.

The next morning, before he went down to breakfast, he put on his newly-issued tan cadet uniform, boots, and sword. He knew that the regiment, in a time-honored tradition, would be coming directly to his house precisely at eight a.m. to escort him to the garrison.

As he was poking at his morning eggs and biscuit, Roxanne finally appeared in the dining room.

"Good morning, everyone," She greeted them stiffly, "Cyrano, may I speak to you for a moment? In private?"

The lump in his throat made another appearance, so he said nothing but immediately followed her into the sitting room. She did not sit down this time.

Don't tell her. Don't tell her, he repeated to himself as he stood next to her. He had to say *something* though. Finally, he knew what, "Roxanne, right now, we are not at war with anyone but that condition could change at any moment. All the things that I have learned over this past year: science, literature, poetry, performing, honor, politics, and even friendship, they are all for naught if I'm not willing to fight for them."

Roxanne did not look at him. Instead, she kept her eyes focused on the floor. "I realize now that I was foolish," she started. Cyrano felt a jab in his chest and moisture forming in the corner of his eyes. She must have seen the hurt in his eyes because she grasped his hands and quickly added, "Not for caring for you. I don't mean that. I shall always care deeply for you. When I say that I am foolish, what I mean is that if you stood in the way of my dream of being a journalist, I would have been furious with you. And now, here I am trying to do the same thing to you, and that is wrong for so many reasons. Most men are fools when they rush off to the army, but I've known you too long to mistake you for a fool. And, well, I see now that this has always been your fate. You have to fulfill this part of your destiny before you can discover what the next part will be."

Cyrano held up a hand in a mock gesture of taking an oath, "I promise I will do my level-headed best not to get killed." He gave her a warm embrace, "We have had some great adventures, you and I. Unfortunately, this one, only Le Bret and I can do." He heaved another large sigh. "I also promise that when I get bored with this adventure, I will trudge home and look for you so we might explore…that next part…together."

Roxanne looked up at him and smiled bravely. "I have something for you."

"Really? What?"

"A going-away present for my brave *Gascon* soldier." From her petticoat, she produced a large white plume for his cavalier hat, which would still be part of his uniform.

Cyrano laughed with delight. "Ah, I have missed this!"

"I told you that I owed you a new one."

"*Mademoiselle*, it will be my signature style." He closed his eyes and bowed gallantly to her.

When he straightened up and opened his eyes, he found that Roxanne had moved much, much closer to him again and this time their eyes locked for a long moment. His heart began to cantor. Once again, he could not resist the temptation to joke away his discomfort.

"Careful! This nose of mine is dangerous."

She cupped his puzzled face in her hands and kissed his nose. She paused for a moment and tilted her head and moved toward his lips.

Just then, they heard the sound of voices; many voices. Men, singing as one, and getting closer.

Cyrano sighed. He took Roxanne's hand again and they walked to the front door of the *château* together. As Cyrano opened it, they beheld an inspiring sight. There, on the green, was Captain Carbon, Le Bret, and the rest of the Guard singing the traditional march hymn of the *Gascons*.

When he saw the door open, Carbon ordered them to stop. He then spun crisply on his heels back to the doorway and saluted Cyrano. "Cadet, are you ready to commence your full commitment to the *Order of Gascon*?"

Cyrano inserted the white plume into his hat, smiled at Roxanne, who kissed him on the cheek. Cyrano turned to Carbon and gave the traditional reply and salute. "*Mon Capitaine*, I am ready to give my life to *Gascon* and France."

"Then close ranks."

He joined into the formation, and the others shouted, "*Vive la France!*"

As he marched away with the rest of the Gascons singing around him, Cyrano saw his entire family standing in the doorway, waving their goodbyes. His chest swelled. He waved one last time to Roxanne, *Au revoir,* dear one, *au revoir*.

Acknowledgements

To Susan, for coping with countless hours of her husband staring into a laptop screen with a smile and a loving look.

To Jason, Cody, and Montana.

Extra special thanks to Samantha for her help, ideas, and pride in her Dad.

This book is also dedicated to all of my fellow Templar Knights and Dames of SMOTJ, nnDnn.

Author Bio

Chevalier **Paul Cicchini**, **M.Ed.**, **Ed.S.**, **NCSP**, the author of *Young Cyrano*, is a nationally-certified school psychologist practicing in New Jersey. He specializes in character education and is the only school psychologist on the East Coast to be certified in the new field of Social Emotional Learning/Character Ed (Rutgers Univ. 2016).

Much like his hero Cyrano de Bergerac, Paul aspires to be a well-rounded Renaissance man. His list of personal accomplishments includes cable television host (*Cars Weekly Video Magazine*-Philadelphia), sports journalist, humorist, adjunct professor, martial artist, fencer, semi-pro football player, high school football coach, collegiate football scout, guidance counselor, Templar Knight (rank of Chevalier), Washington lobbyist for education, webmaster, and author of "The world's first Inspirational-Satire mashup novel." That novel, *GODSMACKED*, was long-listed for the Inspy awards in 2013.

CPSIA information can be obtained
at www.ICGtesting.com
Printed in the USA
BVHW042013240422
635206BV00017B/232